"What _____
she ex_____

"Just being a lord doesn't make you better than anyone else." Alice responded to Lord Rossmore's complaint that people treated him differently because he had a title.

"No, it doesn't," he agreed, distinct amusement in his voice.

Alice flushed. For some reason Lord Rossmore brought out the blunt side of her nature. When he suddenly moved closer, her skin prickled. What now, she wondered warily. You could never tell with this unpredictable man.

"Since you're being so straightforward tonight," he said, "perhaps you'd give me a truthful answer to a very simple question."

Puzzled, Alice looked expectantly at his handsome countenance.

"Would you like to go to bed with me, Miss Alice Lester?"

JOANNA MANSELL finds writing hard work but very addictive. When she's not bashing away at her typewriter, she's usually got her nose buried in a book. She also loves gardening and daydreaming, two pastimes that go together remarkably well. The ambition of this Essex-born author is to write books that people will enjoy reading.

Books by Joanna Mansell

HARLEQUIN PRESENTS
1116—MIRACLE MAN

HARLEQUIN ROMANCE
2836—THE NIGHT IS DARK
2866—SLEEPING TIGER
2894—BLACK DIAMOND

JOANNA MANSELL

lord and master

Harlequin Books

TORONTO • NEW YORK • LONDON
AMSTERDAM • PARIS • SYDNEY • HAMBURG
STOCKHOLM • ATHENS • TOKYO • MILAN

Harlequin Presents first edition January 1989
ISBN 0-373-11139-8

Original hardcover edition published in 1988
by Mills & Boon Limited

CHAPTER ONE

AS ALICE drove along the narrow, deserted country lane, she wished the heater on her old car worked more efficiently. It was the middle of February, and absolutely freezing. An icy wind was howling across the fields, and dark, heavy clouds were threatening driving rain, or even snow.

Anxiously, she glanced at her watch; then she released a small sigh of relief. It was all right, she had plenty of time. She wasn't going to be late for her appointment with Lord Rossmore.

She wondered what he would be like; then she grimaced. An absolute monster, if his reputation was anything to go by! The Helping Hands Agency had already sent two girls in response to the terse phone calls from Rossmore Hall, demanding immediate assistance. The first had left in tears after just a few hours. The second had been made of sterner stuff. She had lasted a couple of days before flouncing out, declaring there was no way she would set foot in the place again!

That was when Alice had reluctantly decided that she had better step in and take over this assignment personally. It was obvious that Lord Rossmore was a real pain, but he wasn't the sort of man she could afford to offend. The Helping Hands Agency was doing well, much better than she had ever envisaged when she had first started it, but she certainly wasn't in a position to displease influential clients. And the current Lord Rossmore was very influential indeed.

She gave another glance at her watch, then pressed her foot a little harder on the accelerator. She wanted to arrive with time to spare, not rush in at the last minute, looking totally flustered. Lord Rossmore had a low enough opinion of the agency as it was. It was her intention to reverse that opinion, to do such a good job that he would recommend the agency in glowing terms to all his friends and acquaintances.

The car bowled along happily for a couple more minutes, but then an ominous clanking suddenly began to sound from under the bonnet.

Alice hurriedly brought the car to a halt and switched off the engine. 'Oh, I don't believe this!' she groaned. She tried the engine again, but the clanking was even worse this time. It was obvious that something fairly drastic had gone wrong, and nothing short of major repair work was going to put it right.

She got out of the car, shivered as the wind hit her with all its full, icy strength, and pulled her coat more tightly around her. Then she gave a grimace. The country lane was totally deserted. No sign of any other cars or people—it looked as if she was stuck here. There weren't even any houses where she could go and telephone for help, just bleak fields and patches of dark woodland. An eerie, empty landscape—Alice shivered again, and this time not entirely from the cold.

She paced up and down a couple of times, trying to figure out what to do. Then, in an uncharacteristic flash of temper, she aimed a frustrated kick at the car. It didn't do any good, of course. She simply hurt her toe; it throbbed painfully for a while as she stood and stared ahead of her, frantically trying to think of some solution to her problem. The only trouble was, there *wasn't* any solution. If she tried to get to Rossmore Hall on foot, she would be hopelessly late. She—and the

Helping Hands Agency—would sink to a new all-time low in Lord Rossmore's estimation.

'What I need is a knight on a white charger,' she muttered gloomily to herself. 'What we've got here is a damsel who's most definitely in distress.'

A gentle nudge from behind made her jump in surprise. She hadn't heard anyone come up behind her. Whirling round to see who it was, she then let out a muffled yelp of alarm as she found herself facing the biggest dog she had ever seen.

Its massive head was as high as her waist, and its dark eyes were fixed on her with a fierce intelligence which completely unnerved her. She wondered if she should make a dash for the car. Then she reluctantly rejected the plan. The dog was only a couple of feet away, and looked capable of moving swiftly and with deadly precision. If it decided to attack her, she wouldn't stand a chance of getting inside the car before those powerful jaws closed around her.

A blur of movement to her left made her gaze swing in that direction. An instant later, she blinked in disbelief, convinced she was seeing double. A second huge dog had slid into view, an exact twin of the first. The same rough, grey coat, incredible size, fierce gaze—and strong jaws——

Alice swallowed hard. This definitely wasn't funny. 'Er—good dogs,' she got out in a quavering voice. 'Nice dogs. I'd really like us to be friends——'

The dogs didn't seem over-impressed by her efforts to get on their right side. They simply stared at her with unblinking eyes, and she had the horrible feeling that they were sizing her up, deciding if she was friend or foe. Then the dog nearest to her took a couple of steps forward, and she felt her knees go weak as it delicately sniffed her hand. She kept very still, but couldn't quite suppress a nervous squeak as its tongue came out to give her fingers a gentle lick.

A sharp whistle suddenly sounded somewhere in the distance, and the two dogs instantly responded, turning their backs on her and loping off. Alice sighed shakily with relief. Then she stared towards the patch of woodland that cast a dark shadow over the far side of the lane. Something was moving through the trees, something very large—and it looked as if it was coming towards her.

Seconds later, a man on a horse cantered out of the shadows, the two massive dogs trotting along just a few yards behind him. Alice began to wonder if she was dreaming. Just minutes ago, she had been wishing a knight on a white charger would come rushing to her rescue. And here he was! All right, so the horse was pale grey , not white, but she wasn't going to quibble over an unimportant little detail like that.

Then she realised that he was most likely the owner of the dogs. Remembering how much they had scared her, an indignant frown crossed her face.

'Do those dogs belong to you?' she demanded. The man simply stared down at her, as if he had no intention of deigning to answer her question. Alice glared right back. *'Do* they?' she repeated angrily.

'The dogs belong to Rossmore Hall,' he answered at last, after a very long pause. His voice was cool and indifferent. Alice decided that it matched his face, which was quite expressionless.

'But right now, they're with you?' she persisted.

He glanced down at the dogs, who were standing quietly beside him, flanking the horse. 'It certainly looks like it,' he agreed. 'But what business is it of yours?'

His sheer effrontery left her nearly—but not quite—speechless. 'What business is it of mine?' she spluttered. 'They came bounding out of those woods and—and *surrounded* me. They're dangerous animals. They should be kept on a leash!'

His gaze revealed a first flicker of irritability. His eyes were dark, she noted. As dark as his hair. And they seemed as cold as his manner towards her.

'Did the dogs harm you in any way?'

'Well—no,' she admitted reluctantly.

'Did they attempt to bite you? To jump up at you?'

'I suppose not,' Alice muttered.

'Then what exactly *did* they do?' he enquired evenly.

'They—they came up to me. And one of them licked my hand.' Even as she said it, she realised how totally ridiculous it sounded.

'That must have been completely terrifying,' the man remarked caustically. 'To have a dog lick your hand!'

'I was certainly very frightened at the time,' she retorted. 'I was completely on my own. If those dogs had attacked me, I couldn't have done a thing about it.'

'But they didn't attack you,' he pointed out in a rather bored tone. 'So why are you making all this fuss over something that didn't even happen?'

Alice could hardly believe her ears. The man was being totally unreasonable!

'I still think you should keep those dogs under some kind of control,' she said furiously.

The corners of his mouth began to signal the beginnings of pure exasperation. A moment later, he turned to the two dogs. 'Romulus. Remus. Sit!' The dogs immediately sat. 'Lie down,' he ordered curtly. They rolled on to their sides, their eyes fixed on him, alertly waiting for further instructions. 'Stand,' said the man, and the dogs gracefully hauled themselves back to their feet. 'Off you go,' he commanded them, and they loped off into the trees, soon disappearing from sight.

The man turned back to Alice. 'Did it seem to you that those dogs were out of control?' he enquired scathingly.

Before she had a chance to answer, he swung his horse round, clearly intending to gallop off after the dogs.

'Wait!' she called out a little frantically. 'Look, I was obviously wrong about the dogs. I'm sorry I made such a fuss.'

'If that's an apology, then I accept it,' the man replied brusquely.

Alice began to bristle all over again. 'It certainly was *not* an apology. I was just willing to admit that I'd made a perfectly understandable mistake. Can't we just forget about the dogs and start over again? The fact is, I need some help. My car's broken down.'

'I'm not a mechanic,' came his curt reply.

Alice stared at him with intense dislike. She was willing to bet that, even if he had been an absolute genius with machinery, he wouldn't have offered to look at her car. Probably didn't want to get those elegant hands of his dirty, she thought with some contempt.

'Is there anywhere around here I could get help?' she asked, hating to have to ask this man for any favours, but at the same time desperate to get to Rossmore Hall in time for her appointment. 'Somewhere that would have a phone I could use?'

'The nearest house is a couple of miles away. And they don't have a phone.'

'Then do you have any suggestions as to what I should do?' she asked with rather sarcastic politeness.

She didn't really expect him to answer. It was obvious that he had absolutely no interest in either her, or her problems. She was sure he was going to simply turn

round and ride off without another word, so she was
definitely surprised when he gave an irritable sigh, then
slid off his horse and walked towards her.

He was taller than she had thought, and very lean,
and he moved with supple ease, as if he was a physically
active man. His features were taut, as if he rarely
relaxed, and as he drew closer she could see his dark
eyes had begun to gleam with bright impatience. She
had the feeling, too, that this wasn't just a reaction to
her; this was a fairly permanent condition, brought on
by the fact that he didn't find his life particularly to his
liking at the moment.

By the time he was actually standing in front of her,
Alice was licking her lips slightly nervously. She hadn't
expected him to have such a powerful presence, and she
found herself wishing he was back on his horse again, a
safe distance away. Then she straightened her shoulders
and lifted her head, a little annoyed with herself for the
feeble-minded way she was reacting. All right, so he was
an extraordinarily attractive man. That didn't mean she
had to crumble at the knees as soon as he came near her!

'Where were you heading, when your car broke
down?' he asked in a terse voice.

'Rossmore Hall.'

Surprise registered briefly in his eyes. Then it
disappeared again.

'The Hall isn't open to the public until the beginning
of April.'

'I know that. I'm not on a sightseeing trip. I've an
appointment with Lord Rossmore—he's expecting me
at eleven o'clock.' Alice looked at her watch, then
groaned. 'That means I've got less than half an hour to
get there.'

His dark gaze was resting on her speculatively now.

'You're from the Helping Hands Agency?'

'Yes, I am. And it's very important I'm not late——'
Her voice trailed away as she realised what he had just
said. 'How did you know I was from the agency?' she
asked in surprise. 'Only Lord Rossmore knew I was
coming——' She stopped abruptly, and stared at the
man standing in front of her, rapidly reaching an
unpleasant but very obvious conclusion. '*You* are Lord
Rossmore?'

'Yes. Which makes you the lady who has so far sent
me two very incompetent women to do what is basically
a very simple job.'

Alice instantly glowered at him. 'No one has ever
complained about their competence before!'

'Then perhaps you'd care to explain why they walked
out after such a short time?'

Forgetting all about the need for tact and diplomacy
in dealing with this man, Alice drew herself up to her
full height and looked him straight in the face. 'When
there are problems like this, we often find it's the
employer's attitude that's at fault, as much as
anything,' she said in a very clear voice.

A second later, she was deeply regretting every word
she had said. She had set out this morning with the firm
intention of persuading Lord Rossmore that the
Helping Hands Agency could supply any staff he might
need, both now and at any future date. She had also
been determined to be so competent and efficient that
he would completely forget about the girls she had sent
him so far, who had proved wildly incapable of dealing
with His Lordship's demands and uncertain
temperament. Yet look what had happened! She had
shouted at him, argued with him, and virtually told him
that he was to blame that those other girls had walked
out on him. Not a very clever thing to do, Alice, she told
herself gloomily. It looked as if Lord Rossmore and the

Helping Hands Agency were about to permanently sever all ties.

Surprisingly, though, he didn't look particularly angry. 'I'm willing to admit that I'm not always a very reasonable man to work for,' he conceded, to her utter astonishment. 'But what makes you think that you can cope any better than the two women you've already sent?'

'I don't flap or panic in a crisis, and I'm very good at organising things,' Alice said with growing confidence. 'And that's basically what you want, isn't it? Someone to deal with the administrative side of running Rossmore Hall?'

'That's exactly what I want,' he agreed. 'As I explained on the phone, the woman who usually runs that side of things has had to go into hospital for an operation. Nothing too serious, but she'll be away for six weeks in all. The Hall re-opens to the public at the beginning of April, and there's a tremendous amount of work to be done before then. Rossmore Hall is more like a business concern than a stately home,' he warned. 'We employ a large number of staff, especially during the summer when the number of visitors to the Hall increases. Its finances are complicated, and there are a large number of problems that you wouldn't encounter in an ordinary company. Do you think you're capable of taking on a job like that?'

His blunt challenge brought a swift and slightly indignant response from her.

'I'm not exactly inexperienced,' she reminded him. 'I set up and now run the Helping Hands Agency, and so far it's been extremely successful.'

One dark eyebrow lifted a fraction of an inch. 'That's rather a matter of opinion,' he commented drily. 'Your track record to date hasn't been exactly impressive as far as I'm concerned. I don't have much choice except to give you a chance, though. I need someone straight away. I can't afford to waste time advertising in the local papers, and then going through a lengthy series of interviews.'

'You won't regret it,' Alice promised him. 'I'm sure you'll find me satisfactory in every way.'

His eyebrow shifted another half an inch upwards. *'Every* way?' he repeated, with a first touch of cool amusement. 'That's a rather rash promise to make, Miss——'

'Lester,' she told him, annoyed to find a brief flush of heat suffusing her face. 'Miss Alice Lester.'

'Well, Miss Lester,' he said gently, 'I suggest we make our way back to Rossmore Hall. Then you'll have a chance to show me just how—satisfactory—you are.'

Alice clamped her mouth shut tight. She had no intention of letting him goad her into another angry or rude reply. All the same, she was beginning to realise why those other girls had walked out. There was something about this man that definitely got under the skin; something about that cool, ironic voice that provoked a hot, flustered response. Did he do it deliberately? She had the feeling that he did; that he derived a certain amount of perverse amusement from watching her trying to control her temper.

It wasn't something that she could worry about right now, though. He was willing to give her a chance, and that was the important thing. She had six weeks to prove she could do the job, and that the agency could live up to its reputation for supplying reliable staff. Like it or not, Lord Rossmore had to have a certain amount of influence around here. The future success of the agency could rely on how well she did over the next few weeks.

She glanced back at her car. 'How am I going to get

to the Hall?' she asked. 'Will you send someone to pick me up?'

'There's no need for that. The horse can easily take the two of us.'

Alice stared at the horse edgily. 'I don't ride.'

'You don't have to. All you've got to do is sit on his back and not fidget around too much.'

'What about my luggage? It's in the back of the car.'

'I'll send someone along later to collect it. And I'll arrange for the car to be towed to the Hall. One of the men might be able to fix it for you.'

Alice wasn't in the least thrilled by the prospect of completing her journey to Rossmore Hall on horseback, but it didn't look as if she had very much choice. Lord Rossmore led the horse over, and easily swung himself on to its back. Then he reached down and held out his hand to her.

For some reason, she was very reluctant to take it. Feeling distinctly uneasy, she finally let him grip hold of her hand, but didn't feel any better once those long, elegant fingers were tightly linked through her own. Then there wasn't time to think about it any more, because her foot was searching for the stirrup, and there was an undignified scramble to get up on to the horse's back.

She finally managed it, then sat there feeling horribly insecure.

'All right?' enquired Lord Rossmore in a slightly bored tone.

Alice grimaced. 'The ground looks an awfully long way away.'

'You can't fall off. Even if you lose your balance, I'll be able to stop you from actually taking a tumble.'

That was true enough. He had one arm on either side of her, lightly supporting her, while his fingers expertly clasped the reins. And she only had to lean back an inch and she would be brushing against his hard, lean body. It made her feel—well, hemmed in, she decided rather nervously, and she hoped it wouldn't take them too long to reach Rossmore Hall.

To her relief, he kept the horse to a steady pace. After a few minutes, the dogs loped out from the trees and trotted along in front of them.

'What kind of dogs are they?' asked Alice, suddenly feeling the need to break the silence between herself and this disconcerting man.

'Irish wolfhounds,' he replied briefly.

'They're a bit—well, big,' Alice remarked. 'Couldn't you have picked something a bit smaller?'

'The dogs aren't mine. I told you, they belong to Rossmore Hall.'

'But you *are* Lord Rossmore,' she pointed out reasonably.

'Unfortunately—yes.'

She blinked in surprise. 'Don't you like being a lord?'

'My God,' he said irritably, 'don't you ever stop asking questions?'

'Sorry,' she responded rather huffily, and she maintained a dignified silence after that.

The horse picked its way across the fields and through stretches of woodland; then it cantered along a deserted road until it reached a wide gateway with large, elaborate wrought-iron gates. Without any apparent directions from the man on its back, it turned smoothly through the open gateway and headed along a drive which wound its way past stands of tall trees. It obviously knew exactly where it was going, and Alice hoped it wasn't going to take too long to get there. She was beginning to feel rather sore and stiff in several uncomfortable places.

Then one last curve in the drive brought them to a wide, circular space flanked by formal lawns, and Alice felt her eyes open very wide.

She had known that Rossmore Hall was one of the largest houses in the area, but she hadn't realised just how big and impressive it actually was. Even in the gloom of a bleak, overcast February morning, the stonework seemed to glow with a golden radiance, and the turrets and domes made an unexpectedly romantic silhouette against the dark grey sky. In full sunlight, it must look absolutely magnificent, and she felt an unexpected pang of envy. It must be marvellous to live in a place like this.

She was still staring round her with a slight sense of awe as the horse came to a halt by the front entrance. Lord Rossmore dismounted, then somehow managed to get her back on to firm ground again without any major mishaps. A man appeared and led the horse away, presumably taking it to stables somewhere round the back, and Lord Rossmore strode towards the ornate archway that led into the house.

Arriving back home didn't seem to have put him into a better frame of mind. In fact, quite the opposite. Alice was vividly aware of a black moodiness radiating out from him as he went up the steep flight of steps, then pushed open the heavily carved wooden door. She didn't understand what was causing that moodiness, though. Surely it wasn't anything she had said or done? All right, so he had been irritated earlier by her nervous chattering, but he had seemed to relax again as soon as she had shut up. But what else could have caused this new darkening of his mood? It had only seemed to sweep over him these last few minutes, as they had approached the house. Surely it couldn't be the house itself that was the cause? Most people would have been thrilled to come home to a place like Rossmore Hall.

Still puzzled, she followed him through the doorway, and found herself standing in a large entrance hall. Two massive statues stood on either side of the entrance, and there was a heavy table at the far end. On it stood a vase of dried flowers that made a splash of muted colour against the wooden panelling behind it. Lord Rossmore was already striding on, though, through an open archway, and Alice scuttled after him.

A few moments later, she stood still and caught her breath. They were in the Great Hall now. Long oriel windows let in wide bands of light, the high ceiling overhead was decorated with painted panels set between dark wooden beams, and huge tapestries brightened the panelling that covered the walls from floor to ceiling. Heavy oak tables were ranged along one wall, there were a dozen or more chairs with plush seats and rigid backs, and on the far side was a massive fireplace with several huge logs in the hearth.

While Alice was still gazing around at all this splendour, a door opened on the far side and a silver-haired man came in.

'Did you have a pleasant ride, my lord?' he asked, slightly deferentially.

'Yes, I did,' Lord Rossmore replied in a curt voice.

The man's gaze flickered across to Alice. 'And will the young lady be staying to lunch, my lord?'

'Yes, she will. You can serve it in the library. She'll be working in there during the day.'

'Certainly, my lord. Will there be anything more?'

'No—thank you.'

The 'thank you' was so obviously tacked on as an afterthought that Alice instantly bristled. Lord Rossmore might have an aristocratic pedigree stretching back centuries, but it was a pity no one had ever taught him basic good manners!

The silver-haired man left, and she turned to face Lord Rossmore.

'Is he one of the full-time staff?' she asked.

'He's the butler.'

'The butler?' she echoed in disbelief. 'I didn't think anyone had butlers nowadays.'

'Frobisher's worked for the family for years.'

'Shouldn't you have introduced me to Mr Frobisher?'

'If you stay, you'll have plenty of opportunities to meet him later. And you address him simply as "Frobisher".'

'That doesn't seem very polite,' she said doubtfully.

His dark eyes glinted with cynical amusement. 'Nevertheless, it's the correct way to address a butler. He'll be most offended if you call him anything else.'

Another small problem suddenly occurred to her, one which she hadn't even thought of before.

'In that case, what do I call you?' she asked. 'Is "Lord Rossmore" the proper form of address?'

'My name is Dominic Seton.'

That blunt statement didn't seem to resolve the problem one way or the other.

'What are you saying?' came her cautious response. 'That I should call you Mr Seton?'

She could see the impatience flaring behind his eyes again, and wondered what she had said to irritate him this time.

'What't wrong with plain "Dominic"?' he growled.

His reply briefly threw her; it had been the very last thing she had been expecting. Right from the moment when she first met him, she had had the impression that he was a man who liked to keep his distance from other people. Yet here he was, suggesting they should move straight on to first-name terms.

'That doesn't seem—quite right,' Alice answered awkwardly at last.

A taunting smile appeared at the corners of his mouth. 'Not respectful enough?' he mocked gently. 'Too informal for a member of the aristocracy? Do you feel inferior to me, Miss Alice Lester? Do you want to bow and scrape to me? Call me by my title? Look respectful every time I deign to talk to you?'

'Certainly not!' Her response was immediate and instinctive and, to her surprise, it seemed to please him.

'Then what are you going to call me?' he challenged softly.

'Well—Dominic, I suppose,' she said, feeling thoroughly uncomfortable. 'If that's what you really want.'

'And I'll call you Alice. If you've no objections, of course,' he added, his tone coloured now with that cool amusement that irritated her so much, because she knew that, underneath, he was having fun at her expense.

'No, I haven't any objections,' she told him rather stiffly.

'Alice,' he said musingly. 'An old-fashioned name. Are you an old-fashioned girl?'

'In what way?' she asked warily.

'How many ways are there?' Again, that faintly mocking smile curled the corners of his mouth. 'Never mind, I don't expect you to answer that. I'm simply saying that you'll fit in around here much better if you leave the twentieth century behind you every time you walk through the gates of the estate. We're only an hour's drive away from London, yet it's like living in another world. I'm literally lord of all I survey. People treat me with so much damned respect that it's almost impossible to hold a normal conversation with them. Some of the old estate workers even doff their caps when they see me.'

'Then why not simply tell them not to do it?' she suggested sensibly.

His dark eyebrows lifted expressively. 'And do you really think they'd take any notice? Oh, the younger generation probably would,' he went on, 'but there aren't many young people around here, it's too quiet for them. They leave to look for work and excitement in the cities—and who can blame them? That leaves just the older generation, and most of them have worked for my family for much of their lives, in one way or another. So did their fathers, grandfathers, and great-grandfathers. They've got such a long history of servitude to the Seton family that it seems bred into them now. Nothing will knock it out of them.'

Alice thought he was probably exaggerating, and wasn't afraid to say so.

'Surely that kind of attitude doesn't really exist any more?' she said briskly. 'Perhaps a few of the older people still live in the past a bit, but I can't believe everyone around here treats you like some kind of feudal overlord.'

'You think not? Stick around for a while, and see for yourself,' he advised slightly grimly. Then his face lightened a little. 'But I get the feeling that you'll be suitably disrespectful,' he went on. 'I think I'm rather looking forward to that, Miss Alice Lester.'

She wasn't at all sure that she liked it when he said her name like that. It sent a funny tingle through her nerve-ends and made her feel—uncomfortable, she decided at last. And not entirely safe.

Dominic Seton glanced at his watch. 'Lunch won't be served for well over an hour yet. Perhaps I'd better take you on a tour of the Hall, to help you get your bearings. It's easy to get lost in a place this size.'

Alice gave a silent groan. She was still aching slightly

from her unexpected encounter with that horse. 'How many rooms are there?'

'About ninety-five,' replied Dominic. 'Give or take a room or two.'

'Ninety-five?' she repeated feebly.

Unexpectedly, he smiled, and Alice's stomach abruptly did a small but definite flip. She had been quite unprepared for that blaze of charm—or her own reaction to it—and was instantly on her guard. Nothing about Dominic Seton was quite what it seemed, and she had the disturbing feeling that you could peel off layer after layer without ever reaching the inner core of the man.

And as she trailed after him as he left the Great Hall, there was a faint quiver of nervous apprehension somewhere in the pit of her stomach.

CHAPTER TWO

By EARLY afternoon, Alice was sitting behind a desk in the library, trying to bring some order to the chaos that surrounded her. Bills and invoices were piled up haphazardly in a tray, there was a mound of letters waiting to be answered, and the accounts books seemed to be in a total mess. It looked as if Dominic Seton's administrative assistant had been away for weeks, not just a few days, and Alice couldn't help thinking that perhaps she wasn't very efficient even when she *was* here.

There were two telephones on her desk, one for the internal extensions and one that was a direct outside line. She hoped that neither of them would ring until she had had a chance to find her feet. As the afternoon wore on, she was very relieved when they both remained silent.

By evening, all the loose papers were tucked away in folders, which she then stacked up in their order of importance. The accounts would have to wait until tomorrow—she wasn't a miracle worker!

Now that she had a few minutes to herself, she looked longingly at the phone. She had been itching to use it all afternoon, and she couldn't fight the temptation any longer. Picking it up, she hurriedly dialled a number that she knew by heart.

It was a couple of minutes before her mother answered it. By that time, Alice's fingers were tapping out a slightly anxious rhythm against the receiver.

'Hello, Mum, it's me,' she said rather breathlessly, as

soon as she heard the familiar voice at the other end. 'I'm just ringing to make sure everything's all right.'

'Alice, you've only been gone for a few hours,' her mother replied patiently. 'What on earth could have gone wrong in that time?'

'Nothing, I suppose,' she admitted wryly. 'It's just that—oh, I can't help worrying. How *are* Tweedledum and Tweedledee?'

'Absolutely fine,' her mother reported. 'They're eating well, and at the moment they're both curled up fast asleep. How's the job going?'

Alice grimaced. 'It definitely isn't going to be easy. It looks as if things have got into a real mess around here. It's going to take me a few days just to get the backlog straightened out.'

'Do you think you're going to stick it for the full six weeks? You're not going to walk out on Lord Rossmore, like those other girls you sent him?'

'I might be tempted, but I'm determined not to give in to it,' she said, with a grin. 'I really need to make a good impression. It could be so important to the agency.' Then she sighed. 'It's going to be the longest six weeks of my life. I'm still not sure I should have come.'

'Don't be silly, Alice,' her mother replied briskly. 'Tweedledum and Tweedledee are fine with me. And with your present financial position, you can't afford to take any chances. Every penny you've got is tied up in that agency.'

'Don't remind me,' she groaned. 'If it fails, I'll be in real trouble.'

'Then just forget about everything else, and concentrate on making a huge success of this assignment.'

'How can I forget about Tweedledum and

Tweedledee?' she said a little indignantly.

'It's rather difficult,' her mother conceded. 'Try
thinking about them *out* of working hours, though.
And you know you can ring me whenever you like. I'm
always here.'

'Thanks, Mum. You know how grateful I am—for
everything. I'd better go now. I don't suppose it would
go down too well if Lord Rossmore found out I was
using this phone for personal calls.'

'Bye, Alice. And remember—don't worry. Just try
and make a good impression on Lord Rossmore, so he'll
recommend the agency to all his friends.'

Alice slowly put down the receiver, then stared at it
wistfully. Tweedledum and Tweedledee—the nicknames she had given to her identical twin sons when
they were babies, and which for a very definite reason
had stuck, even though they were now nearly two. She
hated leaving them, but she had to work in order to
support them. It was the old dilemma of the single
parent. Thank God she had her mother to help provide
a loving and stable home background during the times
she couldn't be there.

An already familiar voice suddenly broke into her
wandering thoughts.

'Do you intend to make many private calls while
you're working for me?'

Alice hastily spun round. Dominic Seton was
standing in the doorway, that cool gaze of his fixed on
her with obvious displeasure.

'I'll pay for the call, of course,' she said nervously. 'I
just needed to—to phone my mother. To—let her know
I'd arrived safely,' she lied, staring back at him edgily,
and wondering just how much of the conversation he
had overheard.

She never openly admitted to any employer that she

had two very young children. Not that she was ashamed of them—she certainly wasn't. It was just that she had learned from experience that there was still a lot of prejudice against working mothers, and people often refused to take on someone in her position because they thought she would be unreliable, always taking time off because of some problem at home. Consequently, she always used the twins' nicknames when working, as a disguise.

Dominic strolled a little further into the room. 'And who are Tweedledum and Tweedledee?' he enquired casually. 'You seemed very concerned about them.'

Alice glanced around rather frantically, searching for inspiration. Then her attention was caught by the two huge wolfhounds who had just followed Dominic into the room.

'Everyone's allowed to have pets, aren't they?' she said in a low voice. 'After all, you've got Romulus and Remus.'

'But they're not mine,' he reminded her. 'I inherited them, along with the Hall. And I had the impression that you didn't like dogs very much, that they frightened you. You certainly made enough fuss when you first met these two.'

'That's only because they're so big,' she countered.

'So what are Tweedledum and Tweedledee? Lap dogs?' came his caustic response.

'They are certainly cuddly,' Alice agreed, slightly evasively. 'And they're still very young, they need a lot of care and attention. That's why my mother's looking after them.'

To her relief, his dark eyes merely looked cynical and not suspicious. 'And do you intend to phone every day to enquire how they're getting on?'

'Of course not. But I'd appreciate it if you'd let me

use the phone every now and then. Apart from anything else, I need to occasionally check with the agency to make sure no major problems have come up. I've already said I'll pay for the calls. Or if you won't agree to that, perhaps you could tell me if there's a public phone nearby I could use?'

Dominic gave a quick shrug of his shoulders, as if he were suddenly bored with the conversation. 'Make all the calls you like. And don't worry about paying for them. I owe so much money already that a few more pounds for phone calls won't make the slightest difference.'

'You're in debt?' Then she flushed heavily. 'Sorry,' she muttered. 'That's a rather personal question.'

'Yes, it is. But it hardly matters. If anyone bothered to give it any serious thought, they'd soon realise my financial position couldn't possibly be healthy. Do you have any idea how much it costs to run a place like this?'

'No,' answered Alice, with complete honesty. 'But from the look of some of the bills on this desk, it's fairly astronomical.'

'Those bills are just the tip of the iceberg,' he told her rather grimly. 'And on top of that I'm having—other problems.'

'Like what?'

For a moment, she thought he was actually going to tell her. Then he turned away, and absently began to give one of the dogs a rough caress.

'It doesn't concern you. You're not going to be here long enough to be involved in any of it.'

But Alice was only half paying attention now. Instead, she was watching with reluctant fascination as his fingers moved rhythmically over the dog's grey fur. The dog looked totally blissful; it was obviously a rare treat to receive this physical attention. To her surprise—

and alarm––she found herself wondering what it would
be like to be on the receiving end of those casual and yet
clearly pleasurable caresses.

Don't be stupid, Alice, she warned herself hurriedly.
There was no point in wandering off into that sort of
daydream. She had come here determined to be efficient
and businesslike, and that was exactly what she intended
to be.

She gestured towards the folders on the desk. 'What
would you like me to deal with first? There are a lot of
outstanding letters—although I'll need some help in
answering most of those—and the accounts are——' She
hesitated, then finished tactfully, 'They're not quite up-
to-date.'

Dominic's eyes glittered appreciatively. 'You *are* an
old-fashioned girl. If you weren't, you'd have been far
less polite, and simply said they're in a hell of a mess.'

'Well—yes, they are,' she agreed with a rueful grin.

'Mary Haversham—the woman you're standing in
for—is a charming lady, and a very efficient secretary in
many ways. Unfortunately, book-keeping seems to be
rather a mystery to her. I can't seem to make her—or a
lot of other people—understand that the consequences
can be rather unpleasant if you don't balance the
outgoings with the incomings,' he finished drily.

'Then I'll tackle the books first thing in the morning,'
Alice promised.

'Good. Are you hungry?'

'Starving,' she admitted.

'Frobisher will bring your meal in a minute.'

Alice was rather disappointed. She didn't like eating
alone. She had been hoping Dominic Seton would join
her for the evening meal.

I suppose that was rather presumptuous of me, she
thought to herself a little wryly. I dare say the Lord of

the Manor doesn't deign to eat with his humble
servants!

'By the way, I'm expecting a very important phone
call this evening,' Dominic went on. 'I'd like you to stay
here and wait for it. When it comes through, go and tell
Frobisher. He'll come and fetch me.'

Alice glanced up, a faint frown shadowing her face.
She had put in a very solid afternoon's work, and it *was*
her first day here. She had been planning to unpack this
evening, and then have a long, relaxing soak in a hot bath.

He obviously noticed her change of expression,
because his face instantly took on that coldness that
could sweep over his features so suddenly.

'When I first got in touch with your agency, I told
you that I needed someone who could be on call twenty-
four hours a day,' he reminded her. 'Virtually all the
full-time staff here work on that basis. This isn't like an
ordinary office, we don't follow a nine-to-five routine.
We work at odd hours, and take our free time whenever
we can, during slack periods. That's why I required
someone who would be prepared to live in.'

'Yes, I understand that,' Alice replied, trying to inject
some enthusiasm into her voice. 'And I've no objections
to working this evening.'

'You won't be working,' Dominic pointed out.
'You'll simply be waiting for a phone call. You can do
whatever you want while you're waiting. Read, knit, sit
and twiddle your thumbs—just don't fall asleep,' he
warned. 'Remember that you want to make a good
impression on me!'

At that, Alice's eyes shot wide open. He had heard
more of her phone call to her mother than she had
realised!

Hurriedly, she tried to recall exactly what she had
said. Then she slowly relaxed again. It didn't matter, he

wasn't really interested. He was just goading her again. All he actually wanted was for her to do her job efficiently, and she was certain she could do that without too many problems.

Dominic left after that, the two dogs trailing faithfully at his heels. They obviously adored him, even though he virtually ignored them, except for a brief caress now and then as an offhanded acknowledgement of their existence. If those dogs had any sense, Alice thought wryly, they would take themselves off and find someone who would love them wholeheartedly in return. Instead, though, they probably spent their days wandering around after Dominic Seton, feeling lost and desolate when he wasn't there, and greeting him ecstatically when he finally returned. 'Dumb animals,' she muttered with some exasperation. Catch her doing something like that!

Frobisher brought her meal on a tray shortly afterwards. Then he immediately left again, with no more than a polite nod. He was clearly a man who didn't believe in unnecessary conversation.

After she had eaten, she got up and wandered around the library, wondering how long she would have to wait for Dominic's phone call to come through. She browsed idly through some of the books, but most of them looked as if they were centuries old, and she didn't dare touch them in case she damaged some fabulously valuable first edition. She had a couple of paperback novels in her luggage, but she had no idea where that had ended up. Presumably someone had collected it from her car by now, but heaven knew where they had taken it. And no one had yet shown her to the bedroom she would be using while staying at the Hall. Although, with ninety-five rooms to choose from, they shouldn't have any problems finding somewhere for her to sleep!

she told herself drily.

It was nearly nine o'clock before the phone finally
rang. When she picked up the receiver, a male voice on
the other end asked for Lord Rossmore. Asking the
caller to hold on while she went to fetch him, Alice
hurried off to search for Frobisher.

It didn't take her long to find him. He was fussing
around at the end of the corridor, and there was a tall,
thin woman standing just behind him, looking equally
flustered. It was clear a minor catastrophe had taken
place. There were pieces of broken vase all over the
floor, early daffodils were scattered around higgledy-
piggledy, and a great puddle of water had spread across
the top of a very expensive-looking table and was now
dripping on to an equally expensive-looking
carpet. Standing nearby, watching all the fuss and not
looking in the least guilty or ashamed, was one of the
wolfhounds. Alice had no idea if it was Romulus or
Remus—she couldn't tell them apart—but from the
look on Frobisher's face, it was very obvious that he
wasn't a dog-lover. If it were left to him, the wolfhounds would have found themselves in a kennel
outside, the house permanently barred to them.

'Er—excuse me,' Alice ventured. 'There's a phone
call for——' She just stopped herself from saying
'Dominic'. If Frobisher didn't approve of the dogs
being given the run of the house, then he certainly
wouldn't approve of such informality. 'There's a call
for Lord Rossmore,' she finished. 'Do you know where
I can find him?'

Frobisher glanced up, looking distinctly harassed.
'Up those stairs,' he said, pointing towards the end of
the corridor, 'then knock on the second door on your
right.'

Alice scuttled off in that direction. Dominic had told

her to send Frobisher to fetch him, but Frobisher clearly had more pressing problems to deal with at the moment. She had the feeling that one of the few things that could upset the usually unflappable Frobisher was damage to any of the precious objects in the house.

She followed his directions, ran up the stairs, and then found herself in a long gallery that seemed to run almost the whole length of the house. Paintings hung all along one wall, while long window on the other side must give spectacular views of the grounds when it was daylight.

There wasn't time to stop and admire anything, though. Instead, she rapped briskly on the second door she came to.

Dominic came out straight away. 'My phone call?' he queried briefly. She had hardly finished nodding before he was off, striding swiftly along the gallery.

'It *must* be important,' Alice murmured to herself. She was about to follow him, but then noticed he had left the door half open. A little ashamed at the way she was blatantly prying, but unable to resist the surge of curiosity that had swept over her, she peeked round the door.

Her eyebrows immediately shot up in astonishment. The room was large and airy, with long windows along one side, and it was almost bare of any furniture. That was hardly surprising, though, because it had been set up as an art studio. Canvases were ranged along a couple of the walls, there was a large easel near the window, and a long bench was covered with brushes, tubes of paint, paint-splashed rags and jars of different liquids.

Alice stared around her a little indignantly. 'So this is how Dominic Seton spends his spare time,' she muttered to herself. 'If he stopped dabbling around with pots of paint and paid more attention to the running of the estate, his finances might not be in such a mess!'

Annoyed that he should have left her sitting in the library for ages, waiting for that phone call, just so he could have a couple of free hours to spend on his hobby, she stalked huffily back downstairs. At the last moment, though, she remembered that it wouldn't be a very good idea to lose her temper. Dominic Seton might be turning out to be an extremely irritating man in many ways, but it was important that she shouldn't do anything to upset him.

As she re-entered the library, Dominic was just replacing the receiver. As he turned to face her, she saw he looked pleased, as if the phone call had brought good news. Personally, though, she didn't care one way or the other. All she wanted right now was a good night's sleep.

'Do you think someone could show me to my room?' she asked politely. 'That is, if you don't want me to do anything more for you tonight?'

His dark eyes gleamed mockingly. 'And what if I told you that I wanted you to put in a couple more hours' work, Miss Alice Lester?'

'Then I'd do it, of course,' she answered stiffly. 'You're my employer. You're entitled to ask me to do whatever you want.'

'What a very obliging girl you are,' murmured Dominic Seton, and somehow he managed to put a whole wealth of meaning into that simple phrase.

Alice turned away slightly, afraid he would see the bright spots of anger on her cheeks. '*Do* you want me to work any more tonight?' she asked curtly.

'No, I don't think so,' he said, to her relief. 'Perhaps I should allow you to get your beauty sleep. Not that you need it,' he added casually. 'It would be hard to improve on your looks.'

His unexpected remark caused Alice to blink in astonishment. What on earth did he mean? All right, so she wasn't downright ugly, but she had never considered her face to be particularly special. Large brown eyes, a neat nose, a fairly ordinary mouth, all framed by dark mahogany-brown hair that fell in uncompromisingly straight and glossy strands to her shoulders.

She glanced at Dominic Seton warily, but he was moving towards the door, as if he had already forgotten about that last comment he had made. He looked back at her, and raised one eyebrow enquiringly. 'I thought you wanted to be shown to your room?'

'Oh—yes——' she muttered, wishing that he didn't have that irritating ability to make her feel totally flustered.

Outside the door, the two wolfhounds were patiently waiting for him. They padded softly along at his heels, and Alice tagged along behind them, third in line. The master of the house and his faithful retinue! she thought with wry amusement, realising what the small procession would look like to an outside observer.

Dominic led her up a wide, curving staircase, then along a corridor that seemed to be leading towards the back of the house. Finally, he came to a halt. 'I've arranged for your things to be put in here for tonight. If you're not comfortable, just tell Mrs Frobisher in the morning. There are a couple more dozen bedrooms you can choose from, if you want to change rooms.'

'Mrs Frobisher—is she a tall, thin woman?' asked Alice.

'Yes, she is. She's Frobisher's wife, of course. She's also the cook, and generally in charge of all the domestic staff.'

'I saw her earlier,' Alice explained. 'There'd been— well, a slight accident with a vase of flowers,' she went on tactfully. 'She was helping Frobisher to clear it up.'

Dominic immediately turned round and frowned at the two dogs. 'Which of the two of you was responsible?' he demanded.

The two wolfhounds stared back at him, their mouths hanging open in big, innocent grins, and their tails waving happily, pleased to have his undivided attention for once.

'Bloody stupid dogs,' he growled, and Alice was amazed to hear an underlying note of affection in his voice. 'Frobisher's running a well-organised campaign to get them banished from the house, and all they keep doing is giving him more ammunition. I swear they're doing it on purpose; they're getting a real kick from seeing how far they can push their luck.' He shot another fierce frown at the dogs, who blithely ignored it; then he turned his back on them and opened the door in front of him. 'This is your room. The bathroom is two doors along to your left. I'll see you in the morning.'

He walked off, the two dogs following him like a couple of huge, dark shadows, leaving Alice to walk into the bedroom.

Once inside, her eyes opened very wide. 'Pretty impressive!' she murmured to herself.

And so it was. The bed was a genuine four-poster, with an ornate canopy and rich velvet hangings. There were a couple of chairs with plush seats, a matching low stool, and a window-seat that was piled high with soft, comfortable cushions. On the far wall was a massive wardrobe and a heavy chest of drawers, and thick rugs covered most of the highly polished wooden floor.

Alice quickly unpacked, the few things she had brought with her looking quite lost in the huge wardrobe. Slipping into a bathrobe, she hurried along to the bathroom, and was relieved to find the plumbing was very modern, despite the antiquity of most things in Rossmore Hall.

Back in her room again, she climbed tiredly into the four-poster bed, hoped that no ghosts would appear out of the ancient walls, and closed her eyes. Just seconds later, she was soundly asleep, and she didn't wake again until the light of day shone through the window.

By nine o'clock, she was back at her desk in the library, determined to spend the day getting the accounts books into some kind of order. She had only just opened the first one, though, when the door opened and Dominic strode in.

His unexpectedly relaxed mood of last night had obviously disappeared. A dark frown shadowed his face, and he scarcely looked at her.

'There are several problems you'd better deal with before you do anything else,' he instructed tersely. 'The toilets are blocked in the west wing, the roof over the south drawing-room has developed a leak, two panes of glass have been smashed in the conservatory, and Remus has been sick in the entrance hall.'

Alice was so busy scribbling it all down that she didn't have time to ask any questions. When she finally glanced up again, she found Dominic had left.

'Well, thanks a lot for telling me what I'm meant to do about this!' she muttered under her breath. Then she reached for the local telephone directory and began flipping through it.

Frobisher brought her lunch on a tray but, apart from that, she didn't see a single person all day. She knew that a house of this size must have a fair number of staff, even in winter, when it wasn't open to the public, but there was no sign of any of them. It was like living in a great, empty museum, and she found it slightly unnerving.

After lunch, she rather guiltily made a quick phone call to her mother. Once she had made sure that everything was all right at home, she gave a brief sigh of relief and settled down to work again.

It was late in the afternoon before Dominic returned to the library. He moved so silently that she didn't even realise he was there until she glanced up and found him standing in front of her. She jumped slightly, then was immediately annoyed with herself for reacting so stupidly. To her relief, though, he didn't seem to notice. Instead, he settled himself down in a chair on the other side of the desk and looked at her thoughtfully for several moments.

'How have you got on with that list of problems I left you this morning?' he enquired at last.

'They're all under control,' she told him calmly. 'A local plumber's coming in the morning to unblock and repair the toilets. He's also going to look at the leaking roof, to see if it's a fractured pipe that's causing the trouble, or if the roof itself needs structural repairs. And a glazier's already been to replace the smashed panes of glass in the conservatory.' She glanced up at him with some curiosity. 'He phoned me this afternoon to say the work was completed. He also said the glass had been broken by someone chucking a couple of large stones through it.'

Dominic's eyes briefly flickered. Then his expression became bland again, and he shrugged. 'Vandalism's always a problem, even in a place like this. There's not a lot you can do about it.'

'What about some kind of security patrol?' she suggested.

'Too expensive. It's cheaper just to repair the occasional damage that's done.'

'If you say so.' She paused, then went on more delicately, 'About Remus's little problem—I mentioned it to Frobisher, and he said he'd find someone to—to take care of it,' she finished tactfully.

Dominic's mouth relaxed into the faintest of smiles. 'I didn't expect him to deal with it in person. Frobisher's got a rather delicate stomach when it comes to things like that—especially where the dogs are concerned.'

Alice couldn't help grinning. 'He certainly didn't look too thrilled when I told him what had happened. He also said he'd arrange for someone called Dawkins to take the dog down to the vet for a check-up, to make sure it was nothing more than a stomach upset.'

'That's Tim Dawkins,' Dominic nodded. 'He's the general handyman around here, and also acts as chauffeur whenever it's necessary. He likes the dogs, and he won't have minded being given that particular job.'

'I don't think Frobisher was actually too worried about Remus's health,' commented Alice with wry amusement. 'He just wanted to make sure there wouldn't be any similar accidents.'

'I'll see Tim Dawkins later, to find out what the vet's verdict was. It's probably just something the dog ate, though. Remus seems to think that everything in this world's edible, providing you chew it for long enough. You wouldn't believe some of the things he's tried to eat.'

'Including daffodils?' asked Alice, remembering the smashed vase of flowers.

'He'll try just about anything. Flowers, chair legs, bits of carpet—he'll wrap those huge jaws of his around the most amazing things. Sometimes I think he does it just to annoy Frobisher. He seems to know how worked up Frobisher gets if anything in the house gets even slightly damaged.'

'Don't you worry about it as well?' asked Alice curiously. 'I mean, just about everything in Rossmore Hall looks as if it's an antique, and probably priceless. I'd have thought you'd have felt a strong sense of responsibility, that you'd have tried to make sure nothing happened to any of it.'

Dominic's face instantly changed, as if she had inadvertently hit a very raw nerve.

'A sense of responsibility?' he repeated in a hard voice. 'I don't think anyone could accuse me of not having that. And the damage the dogs do is absolutely minimal. It's a small price to have to pay for the friendly companionship they give.'

Alice stared at him in sudden comprehension. 'You get lonely in this house?'

An instant later, she regretted she had blurted out that very personal question. It was clear that he had absolutely no intention of answering it. What was more, he had become visibly withdrawn again, as if he intensely resented any prying into his personal life or feelings.

'Forget about the damn dogs,' he ordered curtly. 'Let's get back to more important matters. I realise you've only been here twenty-four hours, but you seem perfectly capable of coping with the work, and you're obviously efficient.'

Alice flushed with pleasure. 'Thank you——' she began.

'But I want to make sure you won't walk out on me during the next six weeks,' he cut in. 'That's why I'd like you to sign this agreement.'

'What kind of agreement is it?' she asked, looking warily at the sheet of paper he had placed on the desk.

'It's a simple contract. It states that, providing you stay the entire six weeks, you'll receive a substantial bonus on top of your agreed salary. If you leave before the six weeks are up, though, I'm not obliged to pay you a single penny.'

Shocked, she got to her feet. 'There's absolutely no need for that kind of contract between us! I'll stay for as long as you need me, I've already agreed to that.'

'But I'd rather make the arrangement legally binding. I'm not an easy man to work for,' he conceded. 'I might say something that'll upset or offend you, and you'll simply pack your things and walk out. I can't afford to have that happen. This is one of our busiest times of the year. There's an enormous amount of work to be got through, and it would be most inconvenient if I suddenly had to try and find a replacement for you.'

'I've already told you, I won't walk out on you,' Alice retorted angrily. 'Why can't you just take my word for it?'

'Because I don't know you very well yet, Miss Alice Lester,' came his soft reply. 'Your word might mean absolutely nothing at all.' He saw the blazing response in her eyes, but coolly ignored it. 'On the other hand,' he went on, 'financial incentives are usually totally reliable. If you had to make a choice between staying and receiving a large bonus, or leaving and being paid nothing at all, I'm sure you'd make the right decision.'

Alice was so furious now she couldn't say a single word. No one she had worked for before had *ever* made such an outrageous demand!

'If you're still undecided, then I'd remind you that there's also the reputation of your agency to consider,' Dominic warned her smoothly. 'I might not be universally liked around here, but my recommendation still carries quite a lot of weight. It certainly wouldn't do your agency any good if I made it known that I was very dissatisfied with the service you offered.'

'You're not a very nice man, Lord Rossmore,' she said icily.

He shrugged. 'So I've been told before. It didn't worry me then, so it's hardly likely to worry me now. Do you intend to sign the contract, Miss Lester?'

She wished with all her heart that she could tear it in half, and then stalk out. Part of her was ready to do just that, and to hell with the consequences. But there was another part that was already whispering words of caution in her ear, reminding her that she could well be throwing away everything she had worked so hard for over the last couple of years.

Hating herself for giving in—and hating him for making her submit to him like this—she finally pulled the sheet of paper towards her, scribbled her name at the bottom, and then angrily shoved it away from her again.

'I think you've made a wise decision,' Dominic Seton told her, his eyes glinting with satisfaction. 'But right from the start I thought you would. You're obviously a level-headed girl, Alice Lester. You're not the sort to indulge in emotional outbursts or futile gestures of defiance. I think you're going to prove quite invaluable over the next few weeks.'

Alice somehow managed to hold her tongue as he picked up the sheet of paper and then left the library. One thing was certain: she was going to be counting the days over the next six weeks, just waiting for the moment when she could walk out of here and turn her back for ever on the impossibly demanding and arrogant Lord Rossmore!

CHAPTER THREE

UNLIKE the previous night, Alice didn't sleep well after she had gone to bed that evening. She tossed and turned for ages then finally heard a distant clock chiming two in the morning. She gave a small groan. She would be fit for nothing tomorrow unless she got some sleep. Staying in bed obviously wasn't going to help, though. The more she closed her eyes and tried to force herself to sleep, the more wide awake she became.

She threw back the covers, pulled on her dressing-gown, and shoved her feet into a pair of slippers. Then she padded over to the window, pulled back one of the heavy curtains and peered out.

The night was overcast, and the grounds which surrounded the Hall were covered with dark patches of heavy shadow. Alice briefly shivered. When she had first arrived at Rossmore Hall, she had deeply envied Dominic Seton for being lucky enough to live in a place like this. After only a couple of days here, though, she wasn't so sure. A place this size needed a large family to fill all the rooms and give them an atmosphere of life and laughter. For just one man on his own, it couldn't be very pleasant, not unless he enjoyed living like a hermit. Perhaps it wasn't so bad in the summer, when it was open to the public and people tramped through in their hundreds every day. But in the winter—Alice shivered again. No, she didn't think she would like to live here permanently in the winter, no matter how splendid and impressive the Hall might be.

She gazed out of the window again, and saw that a few snowflakes were beginning to float down. Then, just below her, something else seemed to move and catch her attention. Straining to see what it was, she peered down at a thick patch of shadow just in front of a large clump of shrubs. She was sure she could see something—or someone—moving around down there. Her eyes began to widen in alarm. Dominic had told her that the Hall occasionally suffered from vandalism. That was probably only kids or teenagers, though, and it wasn't very likely that they would be hanging around at two o'clock in the freezing cold. So who would be lurking out there at this time of night? A burglar?

Alice bit her lip anxiously. What should she do? The best thing, she finally decided rather shakily, was to make sure she wasn't imagining the whole thing. It was difficult to see from up here; she would get a better view from one of the downstairs windows. And, if it turned out her eyes were just playing tricks on her, she could try and find the kitchen while she was down there. Then she could make herself a hot drink, which might help her to get to sleep.

The corridor outside was unlit but, because of the tall windows along one side, it wasn't completely pitch dark. Carefully, she made her way towards the stairs, crept down them, and then headed towards the main drawing-room. From there, she would have a good view of the grounds.

She never even heard the door that opened very quietly behind her. Nor did she have any idea that anyone was approaching her until a hand lightly descended on her shoulder.

Alice instantly let out a loud yelp of fear and alarm. Her heart pounded wildly as she spun round, but then she saw the glitter of eyes that were becoming very familiar.

'What the hell are you doing down here in the dark?' demanded Dominic.

'I thought——' She gulped hard, and tried again. 'I thought I saw someone moving around outside, in the grounds.'

The grip of his fingers tightened a fraction, digging into her skin now. He didn't seem aware of her wincing response, though. 'When?' he questioned tautly.

'Just a few minutes ago. I couldn't sleep,' she explained, her voice steadying slightly now. 'I got up and went to look out of the window, and I was sure I could see something outside. I decided to come down for a closer look, to see if I was right.'

'And what were you planning to do about it, if you *were* right? Tackle this intruder single-handedly?'

'Well, I hadn't thought that far ahead,' Alice admitted. 'Anyway, I could easily have been wrong. It's started snowing, so it's hard to see clearly. Perhaps I just imagined the whole thing.'

'You stay here,' Dominic instructed. 'I'll go and check.'

'I'd rather come with you, if you don't mind. It's a bit—spooky around here on your own,' she confessed rather sheepishly.

'So—Miss Alice Lester reveals a few more of her secrets. She's afraid of the dark,' he mocked gently. Then his tone became more businesslike. 'Stay with me, if you like. But make sure you keep behind me, and don't try anything heroic.'

'Don't worry, I won't!' she assured him fervently.

She followed him down a side passage, which eventually led them to an outside door. Dominic eased it open without making a single sound, then took a step outside. Alice pulled her dressing-gown more tightly around her as a blast of icy air whistled in, then she cautiously peered out.

For several moments, she couldn't see anything except soft swirls of snowflakes. Then she reached out and touched Dominic's arm.

'Over there,' she whispered.

She knew she wasn't mistaken; something was definitely moving by the bushes at the side of the lawn. Dominic visibly tensed as he stared into the darkness. Just a few moments later, though, he relaxed again; then he let out a low whistle.

Alice jumped back in sheer fright as the moving shadow changed direction and headed straight towards them. Then she gave a slightly hysterical giggle as a familiar shape loped out of the steadily thickening snow.

'It's one of the dogs!'

The wolfhound went past her, its rough, damp fur brushing against her bare arm; then it headed off along the corridor, soon disappearing from sight.

Dominic closed and bolted the door. 'It's Romulus,' he said. 'He often stays out late at night.' Even in the unlit corridor, Alice could see the amused smile that hovered around his mouth. 'Remus is a home-lover, he's quite content to spend most of his time inside the Hall, chewing the place to bits. But Romulus has—more primitive desires,' he finished, his voice suddenly shifting a couple of tones deeper. 'They make him restless, he spends a lot of time prowling around the grounds.'

Alice felt a rash of goose-pimples break out on her skin, and wasn't at all certain that it was the cold that was causing them. She seemed to be standing uncomfortably close to Dominic Seton now, and she quickly edged away.

'Perhaps you should——' She cleared her throat nervously, then went on, 'It might be a good idea to get a bitch. Romulus wouldn't be so—er—frustrated,' she muttered, suddenly feeling ridiculously self-conscious. 'And I believe it can be quite profitable, breeding pedigree puppies.'

Dominic raised one eyebrow. 'It's an interesting suggestion,' he said softly. 'And I'm sure Romulus would be behind it one hundred per cent. But the profits on a few puppies would hardly make any difference to the Hall's overall bank balance, and Frobisher would probably quit on the spot if he found out I was planning something like that.'

'I suppose you're right,' Alice conceded. 'Then poor Romulus will just have to go on suffering and taking long walks.'

'His long walks aren't always in vain,' Dominic remarked, with an unexpected grin. 'Several of the local people have got bitches who've produced litters of *very* large puppies.'

Alice grinned back. 'You're lucky they haven't tried to slap a paternity suit on him.' She stifled a yawn. 'I'd better get back to bed. It must be getting late.'

'Getting on for three in the morning,' he agreed.

'You haven't even been to bed yet,' she remarked, realising he was still fully dressed. 'Do you always keep such late hours?'

His eyes seemed to take on an extra gleam. 'Perhaps I'm like Romulus,' he suggested meaningfully. 'Maybe I have trouble with my own rather primitive desires.'

For an instant, Alice's nerves gave a sharp warning twitch. Then common sense came to her rescue, and she gave a snort of pure disbelief. 'Who do you think you're kidding? You're Lord Rossmore—you live in this fabulous house, you're probably a very long way from

being down to your last penny, in spite of all these bills
you keep moaning about, and you're not exactly ugly.
With those sort of qualifications, a man would have to
be really unlucky if he didn't have a whole swarm of
women chasing after him.'

Rather too late, she realised she was being far too
personal. She really had no right to be saying such
things to him. Apprehensively, she shot a quick glance
in his direction, trying to see if he was angry. He didn't
look particularly annoyed, though. In fact, he was
simply standing there and looking at her thoughtfully,
which she found just as unnerving as a quick blast of
temper.

'You certainly believe in speaking your mind, don't
you?' he commented drily at last.

'I'm sorry if I offended you,' she said rather
awkwardly.

He shook his head. 'I like straightforwardness—and
you'd be surprised how rare it is. Too many people
change their attitude towards you as soon as they find
out you've got a title.'

'That's nonsense,' she responded immediately. 'I
mean, just because you're a lord, that doesn't make you
any better than anyone else.'

'No, it doesn't,' he agreed, and this time there was a
distinct hint of amusement in his voice.

Alice flushed slightly. She certainly seemed to be
saying all the wrong things tonight! For some reason,
this man was bringing out the blunt side of her nature. It
was probably because they were still standing in semi-
darkness, she told herself. It was making her say things
she would never blurt out if she could actually see his
face clearly.

Dominic shifted a fraction closer, and her skin
instantly prickled. What now? she wondered warily.

You could never tell with this unpredictable man. He made no attempt to touch her, though, and she gradually relaxed again. There was no need to panic, she told herself. She wasn't going to run into any of those sort of problems. A man like Lord Rossmore wouldn't be interested in someone like her. She could just imagine what his taste in women would be. Someone sophisticated and very experienced; someone who, like himself, had explored the limits of sexual inventiveness, and knew how to play all the bedroom games that such men and women enjoyed.

Perhaps it was because she had begun to feel safe that his next words came as such a shock.

'Since you're being so straightforward tonight, perhaps you'd give me a truthful answer to a very simple question. Would you like to go to bed with me, Miss Alice Lester?'

It was the very last thing she had been expecting him to say. For a few moments she just gaped at him, totally speechless. Then she finally managed to find her voice again.

'Certainly not!' she shot back at him indignantly.

He didn't seem either offended or particularly disappointed. Instead, he simply shrugged. 'I didn't really expect you to say yes. But if you change your mind, let me know. Goodnight.'

'Hey, wait a minute! You can't say something like that, and then just walk away.'

'Why not?'

'Well—you just can't——' Alice finished slightly falteringly, suddenly wishing that she had kept her mouth shut and just let him go.

One dark eyebrow lifted gently. 'I asked a reasonable question, and you answered it. What more is there to say?'

'It didn't seem very reasonable to me!' she retorted.

'Then you must have led an extremely sheltered life,' came his cool response. His gaze studied her in the darkness. 'I find that hard to believe, though. Just as I find it hard to believe no one's asked you anything like that before.'

Alice was glad that there wasn't enough light for him to see the deep flush that had covered her face.

'I didn't say that,' she mumbled. 'It's just that—I didn't expect to hear it from *you*.'

'You mean that a man like me shouldn't want that sort of thing?' A harsh note had suddenly shot through his voice, as if she had just hit a raw nerve somewhere deep inside him.

'What do you mean—a man like you?' she asked, puzzled—and slightly alarmed—by his abrupt change of mood.

'It doesn't matter. Forget it!' he instructed in a dark tone. He began to swing away from her. 'God, I need a drink,' he muttered.

'I'd rather like a drink before I go back to bed,' Alice ventured.

'What do you want?' he asked her tersely. 'A brandy?'

'Oh—no—what I actually had in mind was some hot cocoa,' she admitted.

Dominic stared at her for several seconds. Then he threw back his head and laughed. His response was so unexpected that she gazed at him warily, wondering if he had already had too much to drink tonight. That would certainly explain his odd and unpredictable behaviour. But she had been fairly close to him a couple of times, and she could have sworn there wasn't any smell of alcohol lingering on his breath.

'Hot cocoa,' he repeated, shaking his head now. 'But

if that's what you want——'

His fingers curled lightly but firmly around her upper arm, and she found herself being led along the corridor.

'Where are we going?' she asked, rather apprehensively.

'To the kitchen, of course,' came his amused reply. 'I've offered you a night of passion, and the chance to drown all your sorrows in alcohol. Both offers have been turned down in favour of a mug of cocoa—so that's what you'd better have.'

It seemed to take ages to reach the kitchen, but Alice supposed it took just about for ever to reach anywhere in this vast, rambling house. Finally, Dominic opened a door, propelled her through, and then switched on the lights.

Alice blinked in the sudden brightness. Then her eyebrows shot up. The kitchen was huge! Copper pans hung from the walls, there were massive ovens, spotlessly clean work tops, and a whole host of smaller kitchen implements arranged on shelves. And there was a lot of very modern equipment as well. Dishwashers, microwave ovens, electrical gadgets of every kind—it looked well-enough equipped to be a commercial kitchen.

'Either your staff eat an awful lot, or you entertain half the neighbourhood for dinner every night,' she commented. 'With the help of this lot, you could easily feed an army!'

'We entertain here on a professional basis,' Dominic told her. 'It's a very important part of the Hall's income. Different business concerns and organisations get in touch with us, and ask us to arrange various functions for them. We usually use the Great Hall—it makes an impressive setting, which goes down particularly well with American companies. If it's a more intimate affair, with the company wanting to entertain just a few important clients, then there's a smaller dining-room we can use. It doesn't have the same atmosphere as the Great Hall, of course, but we lay out the family silver and tell Frobisher to be very attentive to the guests that the company want to impress, and it all seems to work out very satisfactorily.'

'Do you do all the catering yourself?'

'It depends on the number of guests. If there aren't too many, then Mrs Frobisher copes with the food, with some help from a couple of part-time staff. If it's a big function, then it's easier—and more economical—to use outside caterers.'

Alice looked at him consideringly. 'It must feel funny, sharing your home with so many strangers,' she said at last.

His gaze instantly darkened. 'Rossmore Hall isn't my home,' came his growled response.

She settled herself down on a nearby stool, then looked up at him. 'That's a funny thing to say. You live here, don't you?'

'Not by choice,' came his abrupt reply. He began opening cupboard doors and searching irritably inside. 'Where's the damn cocoa?'

'Over there,' pointed Alice, spotting it on the shelf. She got up, went over to the large fridge and found some milk, then set out a cup and saucer. 'Do you want some?' she asked.

His grimace was answer enough. Instead, he produced a bunch of keys from his pocket. 'The "open sesame" to the cellar,' he told her, and disappeared through a door at the far end of the kitchen. By the time he returned, Alice had finished making her cocoa and had begun to sip it.

Dominic had a bottle of whisky in his hand. He

opened it, poured himself a generous measure, then looked at her enquiringly. 'Want some? It'll help you sleep.'

She immediately wrinkled her nose. 'No, thanks!' Then she looked at him curiously. 'What did you mean when you said Rossmore Hall wasn't your home?'

He drank most of his whisky before answering her. 'Precisely that.' He lifted his head and looked at her reflectively. 'I'd have thought you'd have known all about our family history. The Seton family are the main subject of gossip around here. I've only got to sneeze, and everyone knows about it in less than an hour.'

'I live quite a few miles away,' Alice explained, 'and we're relative newcomers to the area. My mother only moved down here a couple of years ago, and I came to live with her soon after. On top of that, I've been so busy with the agency that I haven't really had time to pay much attention to local news.' She paused for a moment, then added delicately, 'Of course, I know about the recent tragedy involving your brother.'

Dominic twisted the empty glass in his hand for a few moments, then abruptly refilled it with whisky. 'Not so recent,' he said tersely. 'It's over six months ago now—although it seems like a bloody lifetime,' he added broodingly.

'It was an awful thing to happen,' she said with soft sympathy.

He didn't seem to hear her. 'Bloody young idiot! Throwing away his life for a stupid charity stunt.'

'He couldn't have known that it would go wrong, that the parachute wouldn't open properly.'

'He had no right to risk his life like that! And for what? Not just so the charity would benefit, but to get more publicity for Rossmore Hall, hoping it would draw in more crowds. Well, he got the publicity all night!' Dominic added savagely. 'When the younger son of the Seton family bungles a parachute drop and breaks his neck, it cetainly make the headlines!'

Alice was momentarily horrified by his callousness. Then she realised there was a deep note of pain under the harsh words and she began to understand that he could only come to terms with his loss by getting blazingly angry over it.

'Were you and your brother close?' she asked quietly.

'No, not close. But we understood each other. And, in a way, we complemented each other—probably because we were so unalike.'

Increasingly interested, Alice put down her cocoa and leaned forward slightly. 'In what ways were you different?'

'In just about every way possible. Robert loved Rossmore Hall—the only thing he ever wanted was to spend the rest of his life here.'

Alice frowned. 'And you don't like it here?'

'It's like a bloody prison!' came his growled response.

'Then why do you stay?'

His dark eyes glared at her. 'You don't believe in mincing words, do you?' He fell silent after that for a couple of minutes, and she thought she wasn't going to get an answer to her question. Then he gulped down the second whisky, refilled his glass yet again, and stared broodingly ahead of him.

'Why do I stay here? Because of a promise I once made—and which I never thought I was going to have to keep!'

'A promise—to whom?' prompted Alice, intrigued by the story which was gradually beginning to unravel, offering fascinating glimpses into this man's past.

'To my father.' He took another swallow of the whisky, and Alice eyed him a little uneasily, wondering how much of the bottle he intended to get through. 'Is your own father still alive?' he asked her.

'No. He died several years ago of a heart attack.'

'So did mine,' Dominic said unexpectedly. Then he added, 'Did you miss him?'

'Yes, very much.'

'Then that's where we differ. I hardly missed mine at all. It's difficult to mourn someone you scarcely even knew.'

She looked at him with shocked eyes. 'You must have had some feelings for him.'

'I was aware that there was a blood-tie between us,' Dominic conceded, after a moment's thought. 'And I felt a certain sense of obligation, I suppose. But not much more.'

'Why?'

He shrugged. 'Probably because I saw so little of him. My mother died when Robert was born, and my father suddenly found himself with a young child and a new-born baby on his hands. He didn't know what to do with either of us, so he engaged a nanny to look after us until we were old enough to be packed off to boarding-school. After that, we only came home for the holidays—and sometimes not even then. I didn't mind. Even then, I never particularly wanted to come back to Rossmore Hall. It was very different for Robert, though. He loved the Hall, he absolutely loathed being sent away to school. When he was younger, he sometimes got so homesick that it used to make him physically ill. Later on, he couldn't wait to finish university, so he could live here permanently. Then my father had his heart attack, and Robert and I were both summoned home. Since my father lingered on for several weeks after his first attack, there was plenty of time for some traumatic death-bed scenes. He seemed to realise, rather too late, that there were a lot of things he had neglected to tell us. We were treated to lecture after lecture on the responsibilities and obligations of being the only two surviving heirs of the Seton family. Robert lapped it up—he was a true Seton through and through. I somehow sat through it and endured it, even though most of the lectures were actually aimed at me. I was the eldest son. Legally, it would all be mine after my father had gone. Then my father sprang one final bombshell on us. When he was very near the end, he made us both swear that we would do everything in our power to keep Rossmore Hall in the Seton family, and that for as long as it was possible, there would always be a Seton living here.'

'And you agreed?'

Dominic lifted his shoulders in an oddly helpless gesture. 'What else could I do? The man was dying—and he *was* my father. And I never expected to have to honour that promise. Robert was there, just longing to be given the chance to move into the Hall and run the estate. My father died a couple of days later, and after the funeral I turned the Hall over to Robert and told him he could do whatever he liked with it. I'd have given him the title, too, if it had been possible. Then I set out to live my own life.'

'Doing what?'

He gave her a rather strange look, as if he almost expected her to know. 'I studied art,' he said after a brief pause. 'I travelled—life was fairly pleasant for several years. And Robert was in his element, restoring and running Rossmore Hall. He became engaged, and I knew he'd soon be raising a brood of new young Setons, who'd eventually take over from him. The future seemed secure and settled. Then the damned idiot broke his neck, and the whole set-up just fell to pieces. I wasn't free to get on with my life any longer. I didn't have any choice except to return here and try to take over where Robert had left off.'

There was that note of pain in his voice again as he spoke his brother's name, and Alice guessed at the affection there had been between them, even though they had led such different lives and wanted such different things.

'No one could have forced you to keep your promise,' she said at last, in a low voice. 'It wouldn't have been legally enforceable.'

His eyes instantly blazed angrily. 'I gave my word! That might not mean much to you, but it wasn't something I could just walk away from.'

Alice was startled by his vehemence, but then realised that he was more of a Seton than he cared to admit. Certainly, the family's sense of honour seemed to run deeply in his veins, no matter how much he tried to deny it.

'So you've got to spend the rest of your life doing something you hate,' she said slowly. 'That doesn't seem very fair.'

Dominic's face was deeply shadowed. 'You're very naïve if you think that life's fair.'

Instantly, she shook her head. 'I don't believe that. And I'm certainly not naïve. I was just—sympathising, I suppose,' she finished with a tiny shrug.

'I don't need your sympathy,' he responded sharply. 'I'm old enough—and certainly experienced enough—to deal with my own problems.'

Alice decided she was quite willing to go along with him on that point. She had enough problems of her own to deal with; she didn't need to take on anyone else's.

Her half-finished cup of cocoa had gone cold now. She took it over to the sink, washed it up, then turned back to Dominic. 'I think I'll go to bed now.'

He didn't answer her; he didn't even look at her. She thought he was probably going to stay down here and finish the bottle of whisky, and she was rather relieved. Although making her way through the dark corridors of Rossmore Hall would be quite spooky, she had the feeling that she would feel even more uneasy if Dominic was walking along close behind her.

She had just reached the door when he suddenly got to his feet and strode over to join her. Alice's heart started thumping rather faster, and she looked at him edgily. He stared back at her with that dark, unblinking gaze, and she was the first one to look away.

'I'd better see you to your room,' he told her.

'That's all right,' she assured him hurriedly. 'I'll be fine on my own. You stay here and finish your drink.'

He grinned wolfishly, as if he knew exactly how nervous he made her. 'Afraid of being alone in the dark with me?' he taunted.

'Of course not! I just don't—don't want to put you to any trouble.'

'It's no trouble. Anyway, if I let you wander around on your own, it'll probably be morning before you finally find your way back to your room.'

'I've an excellent sense of direction,' she insisted, a trifle indignantly.

Dominic lounged against the doorway. 'Then tell me precisely how you're going to get there.'

A little frantically, she searched back through her memory. 'You go along this corridor, turn left—no, right,' she quickly corrected herself. 'Then left again, up a small flight of stairs—er—turn right again——' Her voice finally trailed away and she gave a small shrug of defeat. 'OK, I give up,' she said resignedly. 'How *do* I get back to my room?'

'You follow me.' And, with that, he set off at a fast pace through the unlit house.

Alice trotted quickly behind him, knowing that if she lost sight of that tall, dark figure ahead of her, she could wander round for ages trying to get her bearings. Finally, though, they were standing in front of her bedroom door, and she gave a huge sigh of relief.

'Thank you,' she said politely. 'Goodnight.'

Dominic made no effort to move away. Instead, he just stood there, studying her thoughtfully.

'Remember that question I asked you earlier?' he said at length.

She certainly did! Oh, heavens, this wasn't going to turn into a very difficult situation, was it? It was very late, and she was extremely tired now. She definitely didn't want to have to cope with Dominic Seton's amorous and slightly drunken advances.

'I don't suppose you want to change your answer?' came his gentle prompt.

'No,' she said, without hesitation. 'If you think you're going to have trouble sleeping, then I suggest you take the bottle of whisky to bed with you.'

'I'd sooner take you.' His voice was relaxed, rather lazy, and unexpectedly seductive. Alice had the uneasy feeling that it would be only too easy to fall under its compelling spell if she wasn't very careful. 'However, it doesn't look as if I'm going to be given a choice,' Dominic went on regretfully in that same low, dark, velvet tone. 'Consider yourself lucky, Miss Alice Lester, that you've caught me in such an amenable mood. If I were a little more drunk, I probably wouldn't be willing to take no for an answer. On the other hand,' he added musingly, 'if I were a little *less* drunk, I probably wouldn't have asked you in the first place.'

'Are you going to stop waffling on and let me get to

bed?' she demanded edgily.

He gave a slow shrug. 'It's nearly four in the morning and I've had far more whisky than I should—two things which always make me talk too much.'

'Then go and sleep it off,' she retorted, her voice sharp with nerves. She turned round and began to open the door, then felt the briefest of warm touches at the nape of her neck, where a small patch of bare skin showed between her hair and the top of her dressing-gown. She didn't know if it was his finger or his lips that had rested there for that instant, and decided that she didn't *want* to know. Keeping her back firmly turned to him, she shot inside, closed the door behind her, and then leant against it. Since it didn't have a lock, there wasn't any way she could keep him out if he was absolutely determined to follow her inside. She was just counting on the fact that he wasn't really interested; that this was just some slightly drunken game he was playing with her, to amuse himself.

It looked as if she was right. She stood there for several minutes, but the handle didn't turn and there weren't any sounds from the other side of the door. Eventually, she released a soft sigh of relief and crawled tiredly into bed.

The sheets were cold, and she huddled into a small ball, trying to get warm. It had been an extraordinary night, and one that she didn't want to repeat in the future. The last thing she needed right now were any more disturbing encounters with Dominic Seton. She decided that, from now on, she would stick to her bed at night, no matter how hard she found it to sleep, or what suspicious shapes she saw prowling round outside her window. No more creeping through the house in the dark—that way, she should be safe.

Only she couldn't quite get rid of the unsettling im-

pression that no female was entirely safe when Dominic
Seton was around.

CHAPTER FOUR

THE next day, Alice saw very little of the unpredictable Lord Rossmore, which suited her down to the ground. Since there was still a huge backlog of paperwork to be dealt with, she put in a lot of hard work, and, when she managed to grab an odd free hour, she spent it exploring the house and the estate, and chatting to the people she met. She knew that during the summer there would be far more people working here, but she was surprised at how many staff were employed, even at this time of the year. Apart from the Frobishers, there were a couple of full-time gardeners, a farm manager, a groom, the head forester—who was in charge of the large tracts of woodland where trees were commercially grown, and others whom Alice saw only in the distance, going about their business. On top of that, half a dozen local women came in twice a week to clean the house itself. In summer, they would come in every morning, vigorously dusting and polishing everything in sight to get the house ready for its daily opening to the public at one o'clock. In winter, they simply kept the worst of the dirt at bay, only paying special attention to the rooms which were booked by outside organisations for private functions.

Her work was interrupted by a tap at the library door. Then the door opened and a tall, pleasant-looking man in his mid-thirties came in.

'I'm Tim Dawkins,' he introduced himself.

'Oh, yes,' Alice nodded. 'You're the one who's been

looking after Remus and his upset stomach. How is he?'

'I've just taken him to the vet for his final check-up, and he's been given a clean bill of health. Whatever caused it seems to have gone now—one way or the other,' he added with a slight grimace.

'I'm sorry you were landed with the job of clearing up the rather unpleasant consequences,' she said sympathetically.

'I don't mind too much. I'm very fond of the dogs. By the way, I've been having a look at your car, and I think I can fix it. You've got a problem with the carburettor, but it shouldn't be too expensive to put right. You just need a couple of new parts. Would you like me to go ahead with the repair work?'

'I'd really be very grateful,' Alice told him, and that was the truth. Without the use of her car, she was beginning to feel rather trapped. Local transport was virtually non-existent, and the nearby village of Amberleigh was the only place within reasonable walking distance. Even that was part of the estate, though. Around here, it was very difficult to get away from the influence of the Seton family.

Later that day, with the bulk of her work finished, she began to eye the telephone longingly. At last, she couldn't resist the temptation one moment longer. She picked up the receiver and quickly dialled her mother's number.

It was a while before her mother answered, and Alice's forehead began to wrinkle anxiously. Was everything all right? Was there some awful problem she didn't even know about? Her palms grew suddenly damp and panic stirred in her stomach.

Then she heard her mother's calm voice on the other end, and she immediately began to relax again. There couldn't be anything drastically wrong, or her mother wouldn't sound so unflustered.

'Sorry I was so long answering, but I was just settling the twins down for their nap.'

'Are they all right?' questioned Alice fretfully.

'Absolutely bouncing with health,' her mother assured her. 'I'll probably be worn to a shadow by the time you get home again!'

Alice grinned. She knew her mother was loving every minute of it.

'I'm missing them like crazy,' she confessed. 'And my car's broken down, so I can't even dash home for a quick visit if I get really desperate. One of the men here has offered to fix it, but I don't know how long it's going to take.'

They chattered on for several more minutes, her mother patiently answering Alice's non-stop, slightly anxious questions. Then she finally managed to get in a couple of her own.

'Are you going to get any days off?'

'I don't know,' Alice said rather gloomily. 'At the moment, it doesn't look like it. Everyone here seems to work odd hours, and then take time off when they hit a slack period. They still have to be on call, though, in case something turns up unexpectedly. It's all very disorganised, but somehow it seems to work. It means that you never know in advance when you're going to have some free time, though, or how long it's going to last.'

'What's it like, working for Lord Rossmore?' asked her mother with some interest.

Alice wasn't sure how to answer that question. 'It's different,' she said guardedly, at last.

'Have you seen any of his paintings yet?'

There was a puzzled silence from Alice's end. 'There's a sort of studio up on the first floor,' she said finally, 'but I only poked my head round the door, I didn't go right inside. But how did you know he did a bit of painting?'

'Alice, are you pulling my leg?' demanded her mother incredulously.

'Of course not. Anyway, if you want my opinion, he ought to forget about dabbling around with paint for a while. I've been going through the books and, financially, things are pretty bad around here. He should stop wasting time on a hobby, and concentrate on trying to find ways of bringing in more money.'

'My dear girl, he doesn't "dabble around with paint"! And it certainly isn't a hobby. Do you know what it would cost you to have your portrait painted by Dominic Seton?' said her mother with a touch of exasperation.

'No—no, I don't,' she answered uncertainly. 'What are you trying to tell me?'

'Just that you'd have to save up for several years, and even then you probably wouldn't be able to afford it. Alice, the man is *famous*. He's already regarded as one of the foremost portrait painters of the decade. People are queueing up to offer him commissions. And he's not just well known for his portraits, he turns out ravishing landscapes almost as a sideline. I'd give just about anything to own one of them, but they're way out of my price range.'

'Why on earth didn't you tell me all this before I came here?' asked Alice in disbelief.

'There wasn't really any time, everything was so rushed during those few days before you took on this job. Anyway, I assumed you knew. Everyone's heard of Dominic Seton.'

'Everyone except me, apparently,' Alice remarked drily. 'You know I'm an absolute Philistine when it comes to art, Mum.'

'I must say I didn't realise just *how* ignorant you are,' sighed her mother. 'To be honest, I rather envy you. It must be fascinating to be around a man like him.'

'I'm not sure that "fascinating" is quite the right word!' Then she went silent for a moment, her ears pricking up as she heard the distant barking of one of the wolfhounds. 'I'd better go,' she said hurriedly. 'Someone's coming. Give Tweedledum and Tweedledee a kiss from me. Bye, Mum.'

She managed to put down the receiver just seconds before Dominic came into the library. She was well aware that there was a slightly guilty flush on her cheeks, but hoped he would put it down to the fact that the library was very well heated.

'Any letters for me to sign?' he asked offhandedly.

'Just a couple.' She pushed them towards him, and watched as he scrawled his distinctive signature across the bottom. 'And there are several bills, I'm afraid,' she said apologetically.

He made an impatient sound under his breath.

'Most of them aren't too bad,' she went on. 'There's the vet's bill for Remus—he's all right again now, by the way. Then there were a couple more panes of glass to be replaced in the conservatory. I don't know why they keep getting broken,' she added, with a frown. 'Do you suppose it's a couple of local kids slipping in and smashing them?'

'No, not kids,' replied Dominic curtly. 'Leave it with me. I'll see Tim Dawkins and ask him to watch out for anyone acting suspiciously. What other bills are there?'

'One from the plumber who fixed the blocked toilets. Oh, and it *was* a fractured pipe causing that leak in the south drawing-room. He's repaired it, but he said some of the other pipes in that part of the house are in a dodgy condition. If you want him to do something about it, just give him a ring.'

'I can't afford any repairs right now that aren't absolutely necessary.'

Alice glanced out of the window with a frown. There was a light dusting of snow on the ground, and a cold wind was whipping through the trees. 'If the temperature drops much more, those pipes could freeze,' she warned. 'Then you could be in real trouble.'

'I didn't realise you went in for amateur weather forecasting,' he said irritably. 'Why not stick to simple administration? It *is* what I'm paying you for.'

She bit back her own hot-tempered reply, reminding herself that she ought to make allowances for his sudden bursts of moodiness. She knew now that he was in a place he disliked, doing a job he loathed. That was enough to make any man short-tempered from time to time.

'The last bill's from the garage,' she told him. 'They've resprayed the side of your car. Apparently, it was very badly scratched.' She shot him a quick grin. 'Bad driving?' she teased lightly.

Her small joke went down like a ton of bricks. Dominic Seton's dark brows drew together, and his mouth set in an ominous line. Fortunately, one of the wolfhounds came loping in at that moment. It pushed its huge muzzle against Dominic's hand, briefly distracting his attention, and by the time he turned back to her, he seemed to have forgotten her unfortunate remark.

'There'll be a private dinner taking place in the main dining-room tonight,' he told her briefly. 'Make sure you stay away from that part of the house.'

'You don't want the paying guests bumping into

lowly members of staff?' she enquired a little acidly.

His dark gaze swung round and fixed on her. 'You're in an odd mood this afternoon.'

Alice knew he was right. And she also knew why. That phone call to her mother had started up a small ache of longing; all she wanted right now was to be back home with the twins . . .

Firmly, she closed her mind to everything except her immediate surroundings. It was no use thinking like that. She had a job to do, and she had better get on with it. Perhaps, when her car was fixed, she would be able to pop home for a few precious hours. Until then, she had better stop thinking about it, or she would end up in no fit state to cope with the work she had to do.

'I'm sorry,' she said crisply. 'What's the next item on the agenda?'

'There are a couple of minor functions at the Hall tomorrow. A buffet lunch at noon, and members of a local Historical Society are coming for a privately conducted tour in the afternoon. That takes us up to Saturday, when we're putting on a medieval banquet in the Great Hall.'

'Oh, yes, I've got all the arrangements here,' nodded Alice, picking up a folder and flicking through it. 'There'll be three coachloads of guests arriving. An outside organisation's tackling the catering, but they'll be using the kitchens here at the Hall for the actual preparation and cooking of the food.' She looked up brightly. 'It sounds like a lot of fun.'

Dominic merely looked bored. 'That rather depends on your point of view. It's certainly profitable, and that's the only important thing as far as I'm concerned.'

'Do the guests dress up?'

'That's entirely up to them. We hire a vanload of costumes from a theatrical costume company, and set them out in two rooms, one for the women and one for the men. If people want to, they can go in and choose a costume, and then pay extra to hire it for the evening. We take a percentage of the cost of the costume hire, of course.'

'Of course,' she echoed, with a faint smile. 'I'm beginning to realise that everything that goes on around here has to be measured in percentages. Do you usually wear a costume?'

'I don't attend such functions,' he replied briefly.

Alice immediately frowned. 'Oh, but I thought it said in the contract——' She turned over a couple of pages, and then quickly scanned the final sheet. 'Yes, here it is. They've paid an extra fee, on the understanding that Lord Rossmore will be present.'

Dominic took the contract from her, and his face grew positively thunderous as he scanned it. 'Who drew up this damned contract?' he demanded.

'I've no idea. It was all arranged before I arrived. I don't really see that it matters too much now, though. You've signed it, and that's what counts. Either you attend this banquet and collect your appearance fee, or you'll probably have to pay a hefty penalty.'

He tossed the piece of paper on to the desk, and swore vehemently under his breath.

'It's only for one evening,' Alice said placatingly. 'And you'll earn quite a large sum of money from it.'

'By putting myself on public display! What the hell is it that makes someone with a title such an object of interest?'

'I don't know,' Alice confessed. 'Perhaps it's because people associate it with privilege; they think you're someone with a lot of power and influence.'

'Then they're wrong,' Dominic growled.

'Maybe,' she conceded. 'But it's hard to get rid of people's preconceived ideas. Even the staff who work here at the Hall seem to be rather in awe of you. Only——'

'Only what?'

She hesitated, then decided she might as well finish what she had been going to say. 'Well, I got the impression that some of them didn't actually *like* you very much.'

'That's hardly surprising,' Dominic replied, his mouth setting into a rather grim line. 'I'm not my brother Robert, am I? I haven't given my heart and soul to Rossmore Hall, I don't spend every minute of the night and day trying to preserve everything exactly as it is. And of course, most of the people working on the estate come from the village of Amberleigh.'

'What difference does that make?' asked Alice, puzzled.

'I'm not the most popular person in Amberleigh right now. And a few of the locals aren't slow in making their feelings felt in a rather positive way.'

For several moments, Alice didn't have the slightest idea what he was talking about. Then something suddenly clicked inside her head, and she looked at him in dawning awareness. 'The broken glass in the conservatory,' she said slowly. 'And the scratches on your car. They weren't accidents or petty vandalism?'

'No, they damned well weren't. And there have been several other incidents as well,' he confirmed with a black frown. 'All fairly trivial so far, but they could easily get worse.'

'But why?'

He shook his head impatiently. 'Because people around here still seem to live in the last century. They resent any change; they fight it tooth and nail all the way.'

'And you're trying to make radical changes?' Her straight dark brows drew together. 'Is that really necessary? I thought you said your brother had devoted his life to Rossmore Hall. Surely he did a good job of running it?'

Dominic didn't answer straight away, as if he was reluctant to criticise his brother in any way. Eventually, though, he fixed his dark gaze on her. 'Robert's main aim in life was to keep Rossmore Hall exactly as it was. Very reluctantly, he conceded that the house had to be kept open to the public, because that brought in an essential part of the estate's income, but he absolutely refused to go any further than that. No commercialism of any kind, apart from a small tea room and gift shop tucked away at the very back of the house.'

'Well, I suppose you've got to admire that sort of attitude,' Alice commented. 'So many people nowadays can't think of anything except making lots of money.'

'Oh, I admired his attitude,' Dominic agreed grimly. 'What I didn't realise was that it was resulting in financial chaos. It wasn't until I started to go through the books that I discovered just how bad things were. Robert had spent a massive amount of money on repairs and restoration, and there wasn't enough coming in to cover even a fraction of the cost.'

Alice frowned. 'But surely he must have realised that?'

'Robert was an idealist,' Dominic said shortly. 'He saw only what he wanted to see. In this case, it was Rossmore Hall being restored to all its old glory, untainted by the kind of crass commercialism that a lot of the other great houses have had to resort to in order to survive. And the local people liked that, it was exactly what they wanted as well.'

She thought it over for a couple of minutes. 'But surely people realise that the house has to pay its way?' she said at last. 'If they don't, can't you just explain the situation to them?'

'I could,' agreed Dominic tersely. 'But I doubt if it would make the slightest difference. Most of them have got the same blinkered point of view that Robert had—they automatically resist change. They thoroughly approved of the way he ran the estate, and they want me to run it in exactly the same way. When I try to make changes, they let me know in not very subtle ways that they definitely don't like it.'

'But you haven't done anything very controversial so far, have you?'

'Not yet,' he agreed. 'There hasn't been time. All I've done is put the house to good use during the winter months by entertaining here on a professional basis. But it's not enough, it'll make only a very small dent in our overdraft. That's why I've become involved in a fairly radical scheme that could turn our finances around. That phone call the other evening confirmed that it looks like getting off the ground.'

'What are you planning to do?'

'There's a large section of the estate just beyond the village of Amberleigh that isn't used either for farming or forestry. I'm negotiating with a company that wants to lease the land and construct two eighteen-hole golf courses that would be of a high enough standard to attract the major tournaments. There'd also be a club-house with plenty of high-class accommodation, a swimming pool, tennis and squash courts, and a large health centre. If it comes off, the estate will take a percentage of the profits as well as charging them a hefty amount for leasing them the land. It'll make a tremendous difference to our finances.'

'Don't the people of Amberleigh understand that?' she said with a small frown.

Dominic lifted one eyebrow drily. 'I expect they do. But they're still strongly against the entire scheme. They think their village will be overrun by golfers and health fanatics, that people will even start buying up property in the village to use as weekend cottages, which will gradually drive out the locals.'

'Could that happen?'

'It could,' he conceded. 'Although I'll try like hell to stop it happening.'

Alice glanced up at him in surprise. 'You care what happens to them?'

'I appreciate their point of view,' he replied crisply. 'And I feel a certain sense of responsibility towards them. But I'm still determined to go ahead with this scheme, no matter how many bricks they chuck through the conservatory to show their disapproval.'

The phone rang, and by the time she had finished talking to the person at the other end, Dominic had left. Alice thought over what he had told her, and finally decided, rather to her own surprise, that she tended to sympathise with the people of Amberleigh. If she lived in a quiet, picturesque little village that had hardly changed for decades, she certainly wouldn't want a huge sports and leisure complex right on the doorstep. The villagers were right, it had to make a fairly drastic difference to their lives. It wasn't her problem, though. She would be gone from here long before it was finally resolved one way or the other, so she eventually put it out of her mind and got down to some work

On Saturday morning, Alice woke up, yawned sleepily, and decided she would have an extra half-hour in bed. Then she remembered it was the day of the medieval banquet. With a small groan, she hauled herself out from under the covers and padded along to the bathroom. There were bound to be a hundred and one niggling little problems to be dealt with, and no doubt Dominic Seton would expect her to be on hand to cope promptly and efficiently with every one of them.

By lunch time, the cleaning ladies had been through all the rooms that would be used that evening, leaving them absolutely spotless. Later that evening, they would be back to act as serving wenches. Not very youthful serving wenches, Alice admitted to herself with a wry grimace, but they had worked for the estate for a long time, and could be relied upon to turn up punctually and be completely reliable.

As the afternoon wore on and evening approached, she began to feel very satisfied with the way things were going. Everything was running to schedule, and it wouldn't be her fault if the evening wasn't a total success. The theatrical costumes had arrived and had been set out in two rooms adjacent to the Great Hall, the caterers were in the kitchen, preparing the food under Mrs Frobisher's critical eye, and the Hall itself was looking its impressive best.

The first of the coaches arrived as it began to get dark, and Alice gave a sigh of relief. She could sign off now. She planned to take herself off to a quiet part of the house and put her feet up for the rest of the evening.

Just then, Mrs Frobisher came bustling over, a rather worried frown on her face.

'One of the women who was going to help with the serving of the food has gone down with a migraine,' she said. 'That means we're one short, and it's going to make things very difficult.'

'Can't you ring round and get someone else?' suggested Alice.

Mrs Frobisher hesitated. 'It's—it's not easy nowadays to get people to come and work at the Hall,' she admitted at last.

Alice sighed. Drat Dominic Seton, and his ongoing feud with the villagers of Amberleigh! She could do without more problems at this late stage in the day.

'Can't you manage with the women you've got?'

'Even before Mrs Jackson went down with her migraine, we were rather short-staffed. I told Lord Rossmore that, ideally, we needed a couple more women, but he said he couldn't afford the wages.'

'Penny-pincher!' snorted Alice. Then she had to suppress a quick smile as she saw the faint look of shock on Mrs Frobisher's face. Despite the local people's current low opinion of Dominic Seton, it obviously still wasn't the done thing to call him names behind his back.

'I suppose that *you* couldn't help out?' suggested Mrs Frobisher hopefully.

'Me?' echoed Alice, wrinkling her nose unenthusiastically.

'I'm sure we can find a costume to fit you. And it's not very difficult work. I'll explain exactly what you've got to do.'

Although she couldn't remember actually agreeing to do it, Alice soon found herself togged up in a serving wench's outfit. It wasn't exactly elegant, either, she told herself ruefully, surveying her reflection in the mirror. Not for her the rich velvets and bright colours that the guests wore. The square-necked bodice and long skirt were in a rather coarse, sludge-coloured material, worn over a full-sleeved blouse that was tied with a drawstring at the throat. She didn't suppose that hers—or many of the other costumes—were strictly authentic, historically speaking, any more than the food they were going to

serve would reflect a genuine meal of medieval times.
She didn't think anyone would mind, though. The
guests had come here to enjoy themselves; they weren't
going to worry over a trifling little detail like
authenticity!

When she was ready, she hurried along to the kitchen,
ready to receive her instructions from Mrs Frobisher.
Although the actual cooking was being done by staff
from the outside catering organisation, Mrs Frobisher
was still in charge overall. As far as Mrs Frobisher was
concerned, the kitchen was her responsibility, and she
wasn't going to relinquish her authority to anyone.

To Alice, the scene looked like complete chaos, but
Mrs Frobisher seemed satisfied with the way that things
were going. She obviously had everything under
control, and food was already being shunted on to
trays, ready to be carried into the Great Hall.

'You'll be serving the top table,' she instructed Alice,
loading her up with one of the trays. 'Be as quick as you
can, then come back for another tray.'

Alice made her way to the Great Hall but, when she
finally stepped inside, she stopped for a moment to
drink in the scene. The huge hall seemed totally
transformed, full of atmosphere and colour, pulsatingly
alive, instead of just an impressive setting for a lot of
antiques.

She supposed the candles were largely responsible.
There wasn't any artificial lighting, only the flickering
banks of candles along the walls and on the tables. Their
dancing light filled the hall with a muted glow; black
shadows hovered in the corners and the ceiling was lost
in darkness, because their frail brightness couldn't carry
that far.

One table had been set out at the top of the hall, while
long trestles ranged down each side, leaving an empty

square in the centre. Most people had opted to hire a costume for the evening, and they wore a marvellous mixture of styles and colours which glowed dully in the candlelight. The air was smoky and warm, and a noisy babble of voices surrounded her as she made her way towards the top table.

Sitting in the very centre seat was Dominic Seton. The first thing Alice noticed was that he was one of the few who hadn't elected to dress up for the banquet. Instead, he was wearing his usual outfit of jeans, casual shirt and dark leather jacket. 'Spoilsport!' she muttered under her breath. Then her gaze drifted to the people sitting on either side of him. With a faint grin, she wondered if they had paid extra for the privilege of sitting next to Lord Rossmore. She supposed it was the equivalent of sitting at the captain's table on an ocean liner.

Deftly, she slipped a bowl of soup in front of Dominic.

'Your first course, my lord,' she murmured in his ear.

He instantly turned round. 'Alice?' Then he scowled at her. 'What the hell do you think you're doing?'

'At this precise moment, I'm serving your soup. Sorry, can't stop. Some people would like their soup while it's still hot.'

She finished doling it out and, as she left the hall with her empty tray, she was very much aware of Dominic's glowering gaze boring into her back.

When she returned a short while later to collect the empty bowls, he was ready for her. His strong hand clamped round her wrist as she reached out to pick up his untouched soup.

'Is this some sort of joke?'

'Certainly not,' she retorted. 'I expect to be paid for the work I'm doing this evening, the same as everyone else.'

'I'm already paying you an exorbitant wage!'

Alice smiled at him sweetly. 'But this is overtime. By the way,' she went on, 'is that real?'

She pointed at the huge boar's head that sat on a platter just in front of him. Its jaws were wide open, and it had a bright red apple sitting in its mouth.

'No, it's plastic,' Dominic said irritably.

'Thank heavens for that! All the same, it's still enough to put you right off your dinner. Not that you seem to have much appetite, anyway. You haven't touched your soup. Mrs Frobisher won't be very pleased.'

She moved away from him as soon as she had finished speaking so she didn't hear his muttered response. It was back to the kitchen again for the next course; spare ribs in a spicy sauce. Then, hardly pausing for breath, she began refilling the wine glasses and expertly mopping up any spills. As she began whisking away empty plates again, her heavy costume began to cling to her damp skin. It was getting hotter and hotter in the hall, and Alice could feel her skin glowing as she headed back to the kitchen yet again. With a slightly furtive glance around, she poured herself half a glass of wine and gulped it down. It slid easily down her parched throat, and she instantly felt better. Picking up the next course, she waltzed back to the hall.

'Where's Mrs Jackson?' demanded Dominic as she levered a portion of chicken on to his plate.

'She's gone down with a migraine. Mrs Frobisher couldn't get a replacement at such short notice, so she roped me in instead.' Alice glanced up, towards the Minstrels Gallery that ran along the end of the Great Hall. Above the general hubbub, she could hear faint sounds of singing, and it seemed to be coming from behind the intricately carved screen that hid any occupants of the gallery from sight. 'Who on earth is up there?' she asked, intrigued.

'It's the choir from the local Women's Institute,' Dominic growled. 'They're singing a mixture of madrigals and folk songs.'

'Do you have to pay them?' she asked thoughtfully.

'Only travelling expenses. And a donation to their funds.'

'It would be cheaper to have a tape made, and just play that. After all, no one can see them—and hardly anyone can hear them,' she added, having to raise her own voice a little to make herself heard over the noisy chatter that filled the hall.

'Playing a tape would hardly create the same kind of atmosphere,' came Dominic's slightly caustic comment.

'No, it wouldn't,' she agreed. 'But you're the one who's always going on about money—or rather, the lack of it. I'm just trying to suggest ways you can be more economical and make an even bigger profit. Oh, must go,' she went on hurriedly. 'Mrs Frobisher's making frantic signals to me from the doorway.'

Her throat was dry again now. There wasn't anything to drink except the wine, though, so she gulped down a few mouthfuls in between loading up her next tray, then whizzed off with the vegetables.

She noticed that Dominic still hadn't touched much of his food. Nor did it look as if he was making much of an effort to be sociable. As she refilled his wine glass, she murmured in a low voice, 'You'd better start talking to some of these people, or they might decide to ask for their money back!'

His dark eyes glittered angrily. 'Don't lecture me! I won't stand for it.'

Alice was unperturbed. 'Have some more wine,' she

advised. 'It might put you in a better frame of mind.'
Then she scooted off before he had a chance to fling
another bad-tempered retort in her direction.

By the time she was taking round the bowls of fruit
that were the final course and marked the end of the
meal, her feet were aching and she was really looking
foward to getting away from the heat and noise of the
Great Hall. She would have a light supper, she decided,
and then head off to bed. And, since tomorrow was
Sunday, perhaps the lord and master wouldn't mind too
much if she had a lie-in.

She could feel Dominic's gaze resting on her darkly as
she set out the bowls of fruit. It was slightly unnerving,
but she comforted herself with the thought that there
wasn't anything he could actually do, not with so many
people around. When she reached his section of the
table, she slid one of the bowls in front of him, then
hurriedly began to back away. She wasn't quite quick
enough, though. His arm snaked out and caught her
around the waist, and a moment later she found herself
sitting on his lap.

It happened so fast that it made her head whirl. A
second ago, she had been standing on her own two feet.
Now, she was in close contact with a hard, male body
and, since his arm was still firmly locked around her, it
didn't look as if she was going to be able to wriggle free.

'What are you doing?' she muttered. Her face had
gone bright red with sheer embarrassment. All around,
people had turned their heads and were smiling, even
laughing. They obviously thought it was all part of the
evening's entertainment.

'It's one of the advantages of being the Lord of the
Manor,' Dominic murmured in a low voice. 'I'm
allowed the pick of the serving wenches.'

'You're making that up!' she retorted furiously. 'Let

me *go*!'

But he obviously had no intention of doing any such thing. In fact, his other arm had curled round her now, making sure that she didn't have a hope in hell of escaping from him.

'Why are you doing this?' she demanded, although being careful to keep her own voice as low as his own, so the people around them couldn't hear her heated responses.

'I'm simply entering into the spirit of the evening,' came his relaxed reply. 'That *is* what you instructed me to do, isn't it?'

'I told you to be more sociable, not grab hold of me and make me feel like a—a——'

'Like what, Alice?' came his gentle prompt.

But she had already decided that she didn't want to finish that particular sentence. 'No one else has grabbed a serving wench,' she pointed out indignantly.

'That's probably because you're the only one under forty-five,' he told her. 'But a lot of the men are looking as if they're wishing they'd thought of this before I did.' He pulled her a little closer, so that his mouth was unsettlingly close to her ear. 'You are rather gorgeous, Alice,' he murmured appreciatively.

Alice made one brief attempt to get free, but it was useless. 'How much longer are you going to make me sit here?' she asked edgily.

Dominic didn't answer straight away, as if he was thoroughly enjoying having the upper hand. 'Oh—I think for the rest of the evening,' he replied at last.

'What?' she yelped.

'And I don't mind if you keep wriggling around,' he went on, quite unperturbed. 'It really is rather—stimulating,' he finished meaningfully.

Alice's face instantly flared bright red. She sat

absolutely still, tried to ignore the frantic pounding of her heart, and prayed that Dominic Seton would soon grow tired of this game he had decided to play with her.

CHAPTER FIVE

WHEN everyone had finished eating, and the last of the plates had been cleared away, Alice turned her head and looked uneasily at Dominic. 'That's the end of the banquet—are you going to let me go now?'

'It might be the end of the banquet,' he agreed, 'but there's still the entertainment to come.'

'Entertainment?' she repeated apprehensively.

Dominic nodded. 'A couple of semi-professional acts, and a local boy, who's probably going to murder a couple of folk songs.'

'How long is it going to last?'

'I've no idea,' he responded almost cheerfully. 'As long as it takes.'

'But I can't sit here all evening!' she spluttered.

'Why not?' he asked reasonably. 'Have a glass of wine and relax.'

Alice wondered how on earth she was supposed to relax when he was holding her a prisoner on his lap. Perhaps she had better take up his suggestion and have that glass of wine, she told herself through tensely clenched teeth. She definitely needed something to help her get through the rest of the evening!

As she nervously gulped down the last of the wine, half a dozen youngsters ran into the cleared square between the trestle tables. They were all dressed in vivid, chequered costumes, and looked supple and fit.

'They do a tumbling act,' Dominic told her. 'They're not brilliant, but they've got a lot of enthusiasm.'

He was right; the youngsters cartwheeled and somersaulted their way around the hall, until Alice began to feel distinctly dizzy just watching them. Or perhaps it was the wine, she told herself warily. Maybe she had better not have any more.

She instantly recognised the man who came out after the tumbling act. That plain but pleasant face belonged to Tim Dawkins, the estate's general handyman, who had offered to fix her car.

'What's he going to do?' she asked curiously.

'He juggles,' replied Dominic. 'He's a man of many talents,' he added drily.

And he was right. Tim Dawkins did a fast, competent juggling act which brought a lot of applause from everyone, including Alice. Then the hall fell silent again as a young, dark-haired man took the floor, a guitar tucked under his arm.

Alice stared at him, blinked, and then stared again. 'He looks awfully familiar,' she said at last, in a puzzled voice. 'Who is he?'

'I believe he's a local boy, from Amberleigh,' answered Dominic in a voice that had suddenly become devoid of all trace of amusement. 'It's the first time we've used him; I don't even know his name. Tim Dawkins arranges all the entertainment.'

The singer settled himself on a stool and began his first song, competently accompanying himself on the guitar. His voice was deep and pleasant, but there was a fierce set to his features that was at odds with the gentle words of the ballad he was singing.

Alice stared at the young man's dark hair and eyes, and then turned back to Dominic. 'He looks—well, he looks like *you*,' she whispered.

'It's a trick of the light,' Dominic replied tersely.

'Maybe,' Alice agreed doubtfully.

The ballads went down well with the audience, who listened attentively while he was singing solo, and then joined in enthusiastically with the choruses of a couple of well-known songs. The singer finally finished, got to his feet and briefly bowed in acknowledgement of the roar of applause. It looked as if he was going to walk directly out of the hall, but at the last moment he paused and shot a hard, dark glance in Dominic's direction before finally turning and striding out.

Alice was very aware that Dominic had been extremely tense for the last few minutes. She didn't ask any more questions, though. She didn't need to be a mind-reader to know that he had been deeply disturbed by the appearance of this particular young man.

His tension seemed to communicate itself to her, making her feel even more on edge. She poured herself another glass of wine and had almost finished it before she remembered she hadn't meant to drink any more tonight. Oh, well, too late now, she told herself philosophically, and gulped down the last few drops.

The last act turned out to be a fire-eater. It brought the evening to a spectacular end, as tongues of flame skimmed over the man's glistening, near-naked body, and then seemed to disappear right down his throat.

When he had finally left the hall, to tumultuous applause, Alice rather dazedly realised that the evening was over. She was finally free to leave. All around her, people were beginning to get to their feet, and Dominic had released that restricting grip on her now. She got up, took a rather unsteady breath as the floor seemed to shift a fraction, then blinked her eyes, telling herself that it was the smoky atmosphere that was making everything seem a trifle blurred.

'I'll see you to your room,' Dominic told her, slipping one hand under her arm.

Hurriedly, she freed herself again. 'No, you won't. It's—it's not necessary,' she insisted nervously.

'No, it isn't,' he agreed. 'But it'll give me a good excuse for getting out of here.'

She couldn't shake him off as she made her way out of the hall. He was like a dark, rather threatening shadow dogging her heels. Did he intend to go all the way to her bedroom door? she wondered uneasily. It rather looked like it. But what could she do about it?

Absolutely nothing, she concluded gloomily. Trying to argue with Dominic Seton was a pretty futile exercise. She had better just go along with it, say a polite goodnight to him when they got there, and hope that would be an end to it.

The stairs seemed to be a little rocky under her feet, but she managed to negotiate them safely. That last glass of wine had been a big mistake, she realised ruefully. Come the morning—and a thumping headache—she was going to be *very* sorry.

They finally reached the door to her room, and she fumbled around for the handle. Dominic's fingers closed round it at the same time as her own, and then they were somehow opening it together.

'Er—goodnight,' she said nervously. But he wasn't standing beside her any longer. He was already inside the room.

Highly indignant, she followed him inside. Then she instantly realised that was her first major mistake because he immediately closed the door behind her.

'Hey!' she said accusingly. 'I should be on this side of the door, and you should most definitely be on the other side.'

'I like this arrangement far better,' replied Dominic easily.

'Well, I don't!'

'What do you intend to do about it?' came his lazy enquiry.

Alice wasn't at all sure. She was standing with her back against the closed door, and she briefly considered flinging it open and making a run for it. The trouble was, she didn't feel much like running at this particular moment. Her head was uncomfortably woozy, her legs felt none too steady, and her breathing was getting a bit odd, sort of light and shallow.

'Are you going to make a bolt for it, Alice?' Dominic challenged softly. At the same time, he moved a little closer, and her throat began to feel rather funny and tight.

'I—I might,' she stuttered, with a very feeble attempt at defiance.

'Yes, you might,' he agreed. 'But I don't think you will. And do you want to know why?'

Alice was quite sure that she didn't want to know, but she had the awful feeling that he was going to tell her. Then he took yet another step forward and, with a wild fluttering of panic, she realised she had been wrong. He wasn't going to tell her; he was going to *show* her.

She tried to back away, forgetting the door was immediately behind her. The hard wood pressed against her back, cutting off her retreat, and she let out a soft moan of despair.

'Why so nervous?' asked Dominic with a light frown. 'I'm not that intimidating, am I?'

He certainly was intimidating, but that was the very least of her problems right now. This shouldn't be happening at all, it was all wrong, it——

His hand lightly closed over her shoulder, and all other thoughts flew straight out of her whirling head. Oh, that was *nice*; even that briefest of touches had sparked off an instant warm response. Then a sense of reality struggled to the surface, and she gritted her teeth. Don't give in to it, Alice, she warned herself shakily. This man's an expert, and you know all about those, know where this kind of situation can lead.

But Dominic's hand was already unlacing the drawstring at the neck of her blouse. A couple of seconds later, the base of her throat was laid bare, and his fingers were moving appreciatively over the satin warmth of her skin.

A pulse in her throat leapt, and then began to hammer much faster. His fingertips rested against it for a while, as if he was pleased—and perhaps a little surprised—by the force of her response.

'Do you know why I came up here with you tonight?' he murmured.

Alice numbly shook her head.

'Because I thought you'd had too much to drink, and might need some help getting to bed.' His mouth curved into a strange smile. 'Do you need help getting to bed, Alice?'

'No,' she somehow got out in a strangled voice.

'Perhaps you're telling the truth—and perhaps not,' he said in a voice that had taken on a velvet undertone that caused odd vibrations in her nerve-ends. 'I think I'll just go along with my original intention, and see how things progress.'

'I am *not* drunk, I do *not* need help,' she muttered stiffly, ignoring the dizziness that was causing her head to spin and making her sway slightly.

Dominic took no notice. An instant later, he swung her up into his arms. Before she had time to protest, he took three strides across the room, which brought them to the bed. Then she found herself lying on the soft, quilted cover, with Dominic sitting casually beside her.

This was going from bad to worse, she told herself

with a fresh wave of panic. She really had to pull herself together, do something about this before it got completely out of control.

'Do you feel better now you're lying down?' Dominic asked, keeping her pinned to the bed with just the force of that dark, watchful gaze. 'I think the next step is to get you out of that costume,' he decided softly. 'You can't sleep in those ridiculous clothes.'

Her hands fluttered ineffectively against his as he easily found the hooks and eyes. The rough material of the square-necked bodice and the full skirt began to fall away with astonishing speed, and Alice gulped hard as she found herself reduced to a thin blouse and cotton petticoat. How was this happening? She kept meaning to stop it, but here she was, half undressed on the bed, and there was a glitter in Dominic's eyes that hadn't been there only minutes ago. She had seen that glitter before. She knew what it meant, and she *wasn't* going to let it hypnotise her into doing something incredibly stupid.

Only, before she had time to drag all her defences back into place again, Dominic's fingers began to trail along the warm soft skin of her inner arm, and she had to clench her teeth hard together to stop them chattering.

'You like that?' he said softly. 'So do I. And I think there are a lot more things that I'm going to like about you, Alice.'

The sound of his voice seemed to have a very strange effect on her. While he was talking, it totally distracted her from what his hands were doing. It wasn't until he fell silent again that she realised he had unlaced the rest of the blouse. She wasn't wearing anything underneath, and as he slid the thin material aside, one warm, soft breast tumbled free, the pale, perfect skin gleaming

in the mellow light from the lamp that he had switched
on beside the bed.

Dominic's dark head seemed to move involuntarily,
and Alice held her breath and quietly shivered. Except
for that rhythmic trembling, though, she couldn't
move; she couldn't do anything except watch as his
mouth was drawn towards her, slowly but irrevocably.
She knew that his lips were going to close over her
highly sensitive flesh, knew that she ought to be making
frantic efforts to get away from him before it happened,
but instead she just lay there, as if part of her had
already completely surrendered.

And his touch, when it came, was even more
devastating than she had anticipated it would be. Or
maybe it was just that her body had been starved of
these delicious sensations for too long. His mouth
caressed, his tongue gently lapped and teased, until she
couldn't lie still any longer but began to move restlessly,
begging in mute supplication for more, and yet more.

He responded instantly, as if he understood her needs
even better than she did. His hand slid under the soft
cotton of the petticoat, and to the warm caresses that
bathed her breast were added small rivers of pleasure
that ran up and down her inner thighs, forcing choked
sounds of delight past the dry tightness in her throat.
Nor was he so cool now, or so controlled. The warmth
of his breath brushed her skin as his breathing became
faster, and his body was hot against hers where they
touched.

Then Dominic shifted position, at last raising his head
so that she could see his face. His dark eyes were almost
black now and, as she dazedly gazed up into them, she
felt as if she could so easily drown in their fiercely
glittering depths.

'Pretty Alice,' he murmured appreciatively, his

fingers moving again, slowly but with wicked intent, forcing a small gasp from her. 'You might have an old-fashioned name, but there's certainly nothing old-fashioned about you in bed.'

Alice shook her head in confusion, wishing that he would look away from her, stop touching her for a few moments, so she could begin to think straight again. 'I didn't mean——' she began in a shaky voice.

'Nor did I,' he said, with a faint smile. 'Believe it or not, I genuinely meant only to see you to your room. I didn't expect this to happen. But now it has,' he went on in a suddenly huskier tone, 'I think we're going to have to go along with it. There's such a thing as a point of no return.' He moved again, fitting his body against hers, forcing her to share his sudden pulsing response. 'See what you do to me? And you haven't even touched me yet.' His eyes bored down into her, refusing to let her look away, challenging her to deny that the hot flare of desire was mutual.

And, for a long while, she couldn't do it. Her own body had needs too, and tonight it was rebelliously telling her that it wasn't fair she should constantly deny those needs, suppressing them ruthlessly until she had almost convinced herself they no longer existed. In the space of just a few minutes, Dominic had torn aside all the little lies that made life bearable, revealing a passionate nature that still had all its old power to shock her with its forceful demands and uninhibited responses.

Alice shuddered. How easy it was to forget! And how treacherous her body could be, if she gave it a chance. It was so frightening, this side of her nature that she fought so hard to keep locked safely away. It scared her half to death that she could lose control so easily.

Dominic suddenly stared down at her with new intentness. 'You're looking at me as if I've just turned into a devil,' he muttered in a slightly puzzled voice.

A devil? Yes, perhaps that's what he was, she thought to herself a little wildly. Sent here to tempt her, to make her fall into the same trap all over again. Oh God, didn't she ever learn? One night of reckless pleasure—and then years of coping with the consequences. And don't let anyone try to convince her that, as long as you were careful, it couldn't happen. She knew to her cost that it certainly could. And she had twin sons at home to prove it!

The heat was draining fast from her body now and, as her head cleared, she wondered how she could possibly have been stupid enough to have got into this situation. Then, with a fresh rush of apprehension, she wondered how she was going to get out of it. The fires in her own raw nerve-ends had been abruptly doused by the deep-rooted fear of the possible consequences. But Dominic Seton hadn't been touched by that fear; he was still ravaged by the same desires that had stirred her own blood until only seconds ago.

But he was already pulling back a fraction and, with a massive surge of relief, she realised that he wasn't an insensitive man, no matter how many other faults he might have. He had already picked up the clear signals she was giving him. On the other hand, he definitely didn't look pleased. His face had set into hard lines, and his eyes had gone unpleasantly cold.

'Do you do this often?' he enquired in a taut voice. 'Because if you do, you're going to run into deep trouble one day. A lot of men aren't prepared to be—reasonable—when things get this far.'

'I'm sorry,' she muttered. 'I know it's hard on you. I didn't mean——'

'What exactly *did* you mean?' came his harsh demand. 'You're not some naïve little teenager, Alice, so you can't plead ignorance. You knew what you were doing, knew where things were leading. If you didn't want to go along with it, why didn't you just say so at the very beginning?'

She flinched before the fresh blaze of frustrated anger in his eyes. 'I—I'd had too much to drink, I was confused, I——'

'All right, cut the excuses,' he told her curtly, swiftly levering himself off the bed. 'I'm really not interested in hearing them.' He strode over to the door, then paused and shot a fierce glare in her direction. Alice thought he was going to say something more, and she flinched visibly, waiting for the cutting words. Instead, though, his gaze raked over her, as if caught and unwillingly held by the sight of her lying there on the rumpled bed with her clothes still in disarray, revealing tempting patches of bare skin. Then he abruptly turned and went out, and the room suddenly seemed very empty now that it was free of his dominating presence.

Alice wanted to cry, but couldn't. It was as if the tears were bottled up with all the other wildly conflicting emotions churning round inside of her. Instead, she buried her hot face in the pillow, and miserably wished she had never set foot in Rossmore Hall.

In the morning, she had the thumping headache that she had predicted for herself the night before, but at least she was able to think straight again. Not that that was much consolation. Now that she could look back at last night with a clear mind, she was absolutely horrified by what had happened.

Never again! she vowed to herself grimly. From now on, she would be very much on her guard. And that was the last time she would touch wine—or any kind of alcohol. As far as she was concerned, it was lethal. A few drinks, and all her defences just seemed to collapse, leaving her easy prey for any predatory male. And Dominic Seton most definitely fell into that category.

Not that she supposed she had to worry about *him* any more. After last night's fiasco, it was pretty obvious what his next step was going to be. All that remained now was to get it over and done with. She showered and dressed, then ran a comb through the straight, glossy strands of her hair. Her hand hovered over her make-up bag, then moved away again. What was the point? No one was going to bother about the way she looked this morning.

After a while, she took a deep breath, straightened her shoulders and then left the room. Time to face the music.

She couldn't find Dominic, though, and eventually Frobisher informed her that Lord Rossmore had gone out riding. For over an hour she paced around restlessly, waiting for him to return. When she finally saw him cantering back to the house, she gave a dark scowl. Dominic Seton might not like being the titled owner of a magnificent stately home, but he certainly looked like the Lord of the Manor, mounted on that beautiful horse and with those two great wolfhounds loping along just behind.

Shortly afterwards, he came striding into the library. For a few moments, Alice's carefully prepared speech flew straight out of her mind. She felt physically jarred by the sight of him; all of a sudden, she found it oddly difficult to breathe. Then she somehow pulled herself together again. Standing up, she faced him staunchly.

'I thought you'd want to see me this morning,' she said, somehow managing to keep her voice fairly steady.

'Why?' His casual question briefly threw her. While she was trying to work out what was going on inside that complicated mind of his, he added, 'Not that I object to seeing you, of course. You're always a pleasure to look at, Alice. I think I've told you that before.'

She studied him warily from under lowered lashes. What was he doing? Getting his kicks from deliberately baiting her? She decided it would be best to be completely blunt.

'I assume you want me to leave. And straight away.'

To her astonishment, he looked faintly surprised, as if he didn't have the slightest idea what she was talking about. Then his face suddenly cleared, and he gave an amused smile.

'Oh, I get it. You think I'm going to fire you after last night? But that would be a rather medieval attitude, don't you think?' he mocked gently. 'To throw out the hired help just because they won't go to bed with me?'

She could feel the colour burning its way into her cheeks, and hated him for making her feel like this.

'I just thought it would be the—best solution,' she said stiffly.

'But if I fired you, I'd be losing a very efficient administrator,' Dominic pointed out reasonably. 'And where would I find a replacement, at such short notice?'

Alice moved restlessly. Until now, she hadn't realised how much she had been counting on getting away from here, packing her things and leaving Rossmore Hall—and Dominic Seton—far behind her. Now he was telling her that wasn't going to happen, and she wasn't sure how she felt about it. She was beginning to feel so mixed up, and she didn't like that. She was well aware that it was a dangerous situation for her to get into.

'So you want me to stay?' she said slowly.

'You're *going* to stay,' he corrected her. 'You signed a contract—remember?'

She wasn't likely to forget! He held her whole future in the palm of his hand. If she just walked out on him, then he could use his influence to make sure that the reputation of her agency was completely ruined. And she couldn't afford to let that happen. She had too many financial responsibilities, and they were all tied up with the continuing success of her agency.

'Then I'd better get back to work,' came her rather cold response. 'What do you want me to do this morning?'·

Dominic studied her thoughtfully for a couple of minutes, and she inwardly squirmed under the direct force of that dark gaze.

'I'd like you to sit for me,' he said at last. 'I've decided to paint your portrait, Miss Alice Lester.'

It was the last thing on earth she had been expecting him to say. Alice blinked several times, then wondered if he was joking. What possible reason could he have for wanting to paint her?

'I'd—I'd rather not,' she said edgily at last.

'What makes you think that I'm giving you a choice? I employ you,' he reminded her, 'and that gives me the right to tell you what to do during working hours. And this morning, I want you in my studio.'

Alice glared at him. She had never met anyone so unreasonable! He seemed to think he could just order everyone around, and they would do exactly what he wanted. Her flash of defiance didn't last long, though. When it came down to it, all the advantages were on his side. She could do as he said, or walk out—and take the consequences.

'Will it take long?' she muttered unenthusiastically.

'That'll depend entirely on you.'

'What do you mean?'

'How long will it take you to raise a smile? I've no intention of painting you with that dark scowl on your face.'

'Then you'd better try telling me a lot of very funny

jokes,' she informed him. 'Because that's about the only thing that'll make me laugh this morning.'

He gave an unexpected grin. 'The only jokes I know aren't repeatable in female company.' The corners of his mouth curled up even further. 'But I probably know several other ways of bringing a smile to your face,' he told her, letting his tone drop meaningfully.

Not liking the way this conversation was going, Alice quickly got to her feet. 'Let's go on up to your studio. The sooner we start, the sooner this'll be over.'

'You're not exactly falling over with enthusiasm about this, are you?' he remarked, leading the way out of the library.

'I'm not one of your society ladies,' she retorted. 'I don't want to sit for some flashy portrait, just so I can say I've been painted by Dominic Seton.'

His gaze flickered brightly for a moment. 'You don't like my paintings?'

'I've never actually seen any,' she admitted grudgingly. 'I didn't even know who you were, until my mother told me. She's a great fan of yours.'

'But obviously you're not. It doesn't matter, though,' he went on smoothly. 'All you've got to do is sit still and look beautiful.'

Alice grimaced. 'The first will be easy. The second's probably impossible.'

Dominic stopped for a moment. 'Why?'

His question surprised her. 'I'd have thought that was obvious. Either you're beautiful or you're not. And if you're not, then there's nothing in the world that'll alter that fact.'

'Don't you believe it,' he said with a dry smile. 'I've painted women who've had so much plastic surgery that hardly an inch of their original face remains.'

'And did it make them beautiful?'

'In some cases, it improved their outward appearance,' he conceded. Then he added quietly, 'But it didn't give them a face like yours.'

'And what kind of face is that?' she couldn't help asking curiously.

'The kind of face that you could look at for a whole lifetime without getting tired of it.'

His answer astounded her. Seeing the clear shock on her face, he lightly lifted one eyebrow. 'You think I'm lying? Perhaps you're not beautiful in the accepted sense. But you've got perfect colourings—that pale skin with those brown eyes and deep mahogany hair. And your bone structure is fascinating—interesting lines, a delicate silhouette, but with an underlying strength. As for your mouth—I could spend a whole week painting your mouth, and thoroughly enjoy every minute,' he finished slightly huskily.

Alice felt totally embarrassed now, and more than a little uncomfortable. 'Let's hope it doesn't take that long,' she muttered edgily. 'I've got a lot of work to get on with.'

She set off along the corridor at a brisk pace, but Dominic easily kept up with her. She could hear their two sets of footsteps echoing through the deserted corridors, and she gave a faint frown.

'This place always seems so empty. I suppose it's better in the summer, when it's open to the public and there are loads of people tramping through.'

Dominic shrugged. 'In the summer, there's no privacy. In the winter, the house seems completely lifeless. You take your pick which you prefer.'

'Which would you choose?'

'Neither,' he replied tersely. 'This isn't my home, I don't want to be here.'

Alice's brows drew together. 'But since you haven't

got a choice, perhaps you ought to try and do something about it.'

'Such as?'

'Well—the most obvious solution would be to get married and fill the place with a noisy horde of kids. That would certainly solve the problem of the place being too quiet!'

'No.'

His curt answer—and, more than that, the almost dangerously quiet tone of his voice—made her shoot a puzzled glance at him.

'What do you mean—no?'

'I'd have thought it was perfectly clear.' His tone had gone quite icy now, obviously warning against any further questions on the subject. Alice wasn't put off that easily, though.

'It's not very clear to me.'

He shot a stormy glance at her. 'Then I'll spell it out for you. No marriage. No kids. It's a decision I made a long time ago, and something I shan't change my mind over.'

'A lot of people say that,' she agreed. 'And I suppose a bachelor existence is very appealing to a man like you. But one day something will probably happen to make you change your mind——'

'Alice, drop it!'

And this time he finally got through to her. Realising she had hit a nerve that, for some unknown reason, was scraped nearly raw, she obediently shut up. Yet she couldn't help wondering what had prompted that almost savage response from him.

None of your business, Alice, she reminded herself. All the same, she couldn't quite get it out of her mind, and she didn't entirely stop thinking about it until they finally reached the studio.

It was just as she remembered it from that day when she had first peeped round the door, except that this morning it was filled with clear daylight streaming in through the long windows. While she wandered around, examining the studio with new interest, Dominic set up a plain wooden chair at the far end.

'Sit here,' he instructed. 'This morning I'll just do some preliminary sketches. When I get round to the actual painting, I'll probably want you to wear something fairly rich—velvet, perhaps—and in a deep shade that'll bring out your own colourings, make them even more dramatic.'

Alice settled herself on the chair, then glanced up slightly nervously as he came over to her and stood very close.

'I want you to put your head at this angle——' one of his fingers gently came up under her chin and raised it a couple of inches '—and let your hands lie loose in your lap, like this.'

His own hands closed round her wrists as he made the adjustments he wanted, and she felt herself instinctively stiffen. His touch was quite impersonal, but it was enough to bring memories of last night rushing back into her head. She tried to force them out again, but it was far more difficult than she would have liked, and she had the uncomfortable feeling that he knew it. She kept her eyes averted from him, but was very aware that he was looking at her with sharp thoughtfulness.

'Why are you pretending you don't like being touched?' he asked at last. 'Because you *do* like it. You like it a lot.' He deliberately allowed one warm fingertip to trail from her wrist to the open palm of her hand, and her fingers involuntarily shook at that light contact.

'Do you want to get on with this painting, or play silly games?' she got out in a forced voice.

His mouth relaxed into a slightly mocking grin. 'I'd have thought the answer to that was fairly obvious. But I suppose I should get on with the drawings before the light begins to go.'

Feeling jumpy and on edge, Alice sat tensely in the chair and hoped this wouldn't take too long. She wasn't sure her frayed nerves could cope with Dominic Seton for more than short stretches at a time!

CHAPTER SIX

DOMINIC settled himself down a few feet away, and then began quickly sketching. Alice found it completely unnerving to have that dark gaze flicking over her every few seconds, running assessingly over her features, the open eye contact somehow even more intimate than a physical touch.

To try and distract herself from her nervousness, she blurted out, 'Can I talk while you're drawing?'

'As long as you don't move any part of you except your mouth,' he answered easily.

The trouble was, she couldn't think of a single topic of conversation. At least, not one that was safely impersonal. And she definitely didn't want to stray on to any subject that would cause even more friction between them. This whole situation was already difficult enough; she needed to chatter about something soothing—like the weather.

'It's very cold out. Do you think it's going to snow?' she ventured.

'No.'

Since he didn't volunteer any more than that one word, that seemed to put an end to that particular topic of conversation. She was rather frantically trying to think of another one when he briefly raised his head. 'How did you start your agency?' he asked.

She hadn't been expecting that question, so it was quite a while before she collected her thoughts together and answered him.

'I'd been living and working in London for a couple of years, but——' She hesitated, and chose her next words very carefully. 'Circumstances changed, and I had to give up my job, so my mother suggested I should go and live with her for a while, until—until I'd got my life sorted out again. She'd recently moved to this area, and she'd been lonely since my father died. It seemed like the ideal solution. The only trouble was, it was hard to find work around here.'

Dominic nodded. 'It's one of the great drawbacks of an area that's still very rural.'

'I started looking into it more deeply, and I found there *was* work, but much of it was part-time. Small local firms wanted temporary replacements for staff on holiday, shops needed girls who would stand in at short notice for people who'd gone sick, that sort of thing. Then I found it went further than that. There were old people who needed gardeners or decorators, young mothers who were desperate for baby-sitters, people looking after elderly relatives who needed someone to take over occasionally so they could have a much-needed break—the list really seemed endless.'

'So you decided to do something about it?'

'It seemed like a good idea, because there are a lot of people around here who actually prefer part-time work. Mothers with kids at school, which means they can only work in term-time, people who have taken early retirement and want a job that takes up just a couple of days each week. It was just a question of matching them all together. And, of course, we supply full-time staff as well. Now that the agency's getting known, more and more local companies are getting in touch with us when they've got vacancies.'

'You make it sound fairly straightforward,' Dominic said, lightly raising one eyebrow. 'But my guess is that it wasn't at all easy to set up.'

'No, it wasn't,' she agreed with a grimace, remembering all the set-backs, the problems, the times she had been tempted to give up. 'But it's running fairly smoothly now, and there's a local girl, Susie, who takes over when I'm not there. She's marvellously efficient, she keeps everything going if I have to go out on a job personally.'

'It sounds like a busy life,' he commented. 'But is it a lonely one, as well?'

'What do you mean?' she asked with sudden wariness, wondering where this line of questioning was leading.

'You've talked a lot about work, but not once mentioned your personal life. Do you have one?'

'I don't see that's any business of yours!' Her tone was sharp as she tried to cover up the fact that she was beginning to feel flustered. 'Anyway, I could say the same thing about you. You own this huge great house, but I haven't seen any signs of friends dropping in, and social events are pretty thin on the ground—apart from the ones people are willing to pay for, of course,' she added with a touch of sarcasm. 'Or do you only invite people here if they pay for the privilege?'

His dark brows drew together in a warning frown. 'Perhaps I just don't fit into the social scene around here.'

Alice looked at him assessingly. 'That's a bit hard to believe,' she said at last. 'You're a Seton, aren't you? You can trace your ancestors back for generations, and you've got their portraits stuck all over the walls to prove it. Not only that, but you're the owner of one of the finest houses around here. *And* you're a famous painter. That's got to make you one of the most eligible men in this part of the country. By rights, you ought to be at the top of everyone's invitation list.'

'If you ignore the invitations for long enough, eventually they stop coming.'

'Aren't you interested in mixing socially?'

'With people with whom I've nothing in common? No.'

Alice studied him thoughtfully. 'You must be a great disappointment to all the mothers with marriageable daughters,' she remarked at last. 'They're probably itching for the opportunity to parade all their gorgeous offspring in front of you, and you're not interested, you won't give them a chance.'

Dominic shot her a mocking glance. 'I didn't say I wasn't interested. Only that I've no intention of getting married. I thought I'd made it perfectly clear that I'm *very* interested in the female sex.'

Something in his velvet tone reminded her only too vividly of what had happened between them last night, and a light flush threatened to cover her face. She hurriedly fought it back, then gabbled on nervously to hide her confusion.

'All the same, I suppose you're going to have to think about marriage one day. There's the title, this house and all the land—I know you didn't want any of it, but now you've got it, I suppose you're eventually going to have to produce a son and heir to inherit it all.'

An instant later, Dominic's pencil flew across the room, cracking against the far wall with a sharp sound that made her jump. His sketching-pad was already flung down to the floor, and his face had abruptly grown thunderous.

'Are there any more highly personal questions you'd like to ask me?' he demanded, glaring at her fiercely.

'I—I'm sorry, I didn't mean——' she began stutteringly, instinctively drawing back from this sudden blaze of sheer temper.

'Yes, you *did* mean! But, since you're so interested in my private life, let's get a few things straight, once and for all. I don't intend to marry, and I don't intend to have children. Because of the promise I made to my father, I'm tied to this damned house for the rest of my life, but once I'm dead there'll be no more Setons at Rossmore Hall. So, if you're nursing any hopes of catching a titled husband for yourself, forget them! I might have wanted you in my bed last night—I might still want you there right now,' he went on, his eyes flaring brightly as they drank in the sight of her, 'but that's as far as it goes. Am I making myself clear?'

Totally stunned, Alice just stared at him, white-faced, for several seconds. Then she got to her feet and shot him a completely contemptuous look.

'Perfectly clear,' she said icily. 'But that little speech wasn't necessary. As it happens, I'm not looking for a husband. Like you, I'm not interested in marriage. But even if I were, I certainly wouldn't consider a rude and foul-tempered man such as you, Lord Rossmore!'

With that, she stalked out of the studio with as much dignity as she could muster.

Ten minutes later, she was still shaking with reaction. That sudden flare-up between them had disturbed her far more than she cared to admit, and it was all the more unsettling because she didn't even really understand what had caused it. All right, so she had asked a lot of questions. If he hadn't liked it, though, why hadn't he simply asked her to stop? There had been no need for him to tear into her like that.

As her nervous system gradually steadied, she gave a small sigh and got to her feet. She had returned to her bedroom, and now she walked over to the wardrobe and began to take out her clothes. He would hardly want her to stay here after that ugly little scene, so she had better pack and get out as quickly as she could.

She had just finished piling skirts and jumpers on to the bed when there was a brief rap on the door. Then, without waiting for her to invite him in, Dominic opened it and strode inside.

'Come to make sure I'm leaving?' she enquired with acerbity. 'Well, don't worry. I'm packing as fast as I can.'

Dominic fixed his dark gaze on her thoughtfully. 'I didn't think you'd run away just because I shouted at you,' he commented at last. 'I thought you had more guts than that.'

'It wasn't—I'm not scared of you——' Alice swallowed hard, then tried again. 'I can cope with your bad temper,' she said evenly. 'What I *didn't* like was what you said.'

'You're walking out on me because I accused you of being a fortune-hunter?' His mouth set into a wry line. 'I often say things I don't mean. I thought you were intelligent enough to realise that.'

'I'm not stupid, but neither am I a mind-reader,' Alice replied stiffly.

'But I think you're beginning to understand me a little,' he said softly, and seemed pleased when she didn't flatly contradict him. He was silent for a few more moments; then he held something out to her. It was a flat package, just over a foot square.

She stared at it guardedly. 'What is it?'

'A painting. I'd like you to have it.'

'I don't want it,' she replied at once.

His gaze hardened noticeably. 'Why not?'

'Because your paintings are valuable. I couldn't accept something like that. It would be like—well, like taking a bribe.'

'And what exactly do you think I'm trying to bribe you to do?' came his slightly mocking challenge.

'I don't know,' she admitted, shifting around a little restlessly. 'I just—don't feel comfortable about it.'

'As a matter of fact, the painting isn't for you,' he told her, to her surprise. 'It's for your mother. You did say she was a fan of mine, didn't you?'

'Yes—I did,' she stuttered. 'She'd give her right arm for one of your paintings. But——' She fell silent, realising how cleverly he had boxed her into this difficult situation.

'I think you should take it,' Dominic said, with a trace of amusement. 'It's by way of an apology—and it's the only one you're likely to get. You're right, I've got a filthy temper, and it gets out of hand at times. But it never lasts for very long, and I always regret it afterwards. And sometimes—like today—I even try to make amends.'

What could she do except take the package from him? When he turned on the charm like that, it was virtually impossible to resist him for long. And, anyway, her mother would get such tremendous pleasure from the painting. Alice was very much aware that she owed her mother so much. To be able to give her a painting by Dominic Seton would go just a little way towards repaying that tremendous debt.

'Thank you,' she muttered. Then she added, 'Can I look at it?'

'If you like.'

She took off the brown paper, and instantly the small painting seemed to blaze up at her, a dazzling combination of colour and clear, almost luminous light. It was a simple scene: mountains and trees and brilliant patches of wild flowers, with a hilltop town in the distance, a huddle of houses with red-tiled roofs and glowing amber walls, clinging precariously to the steep slopes. Alice could almost feel the warmth of the sun beating down from the clear blue sky, share the peaceful, lazy way of life of the people who lived in that age-old town.

'Where is it?' she asked, staring at it in fascination.

'Provence, in the south of France,' he replied. 'It's the view from the window of my house there.'

'Your house?' echoed Alice.

'I told you that this place wasn't my home. Whenever I've got some free time, this is where I go—where I used to go,' he corrected himself, with a brief frown. 'It's an old, converted farmhouse, far enough off the beaten track so no tourists ever find their way there, but little more than an hour's drive from the Côte d'Azur if things ever get *too* quiet.'

'It looks gorgeous,' she said wistfully.

'Come and see it for yourself one day,' Dominic invited, his dark eyes fixing on her with a curiously cool expression that made it hard for her to decide if he was joking or not.

Alice gave an uncertain smile. 'Perhaps I will,' she said equally offhandedly. And, since he didn't press her for a more definite answer, she decided that it was just a very casual invitation that didn't actually mean anything.

Eventually—and much to her relief—he released her from the dark, steady inspection of those disturbing eyes. Instead, his gaze fixed on the heap of clothes on the bed.

'Am I forgiven?' he enquired, raising one eyebrow slightly mockingly. 'Are you going to put those back in the wardrobe now?'

'I suppose so,' she conceded grudgingly. Then, with a

severe glance in his direction, she added, 'You really are a very difficult man to work for.'

'I warned you that I would be.'

'Yes, I know. But I didn't expect——'

'Didn't expect what?' he prompted gently.

She flushed slightly. 'Never mind.' She picked up her clothes and began to shovel them back into the cupboards.

Dominic walked towards the door, then paused. 'By the way, I was talking to Tim Dawkins this morning, and he told me he's fixed your car. You shouldn't have any more problems with it.'

Alice's head came up at once. 'In that case, could I—could I have the afternoon off?' Her eyes sparkled hopefully as she waited for his answer, and she hoped he couldn't see her fingers crossed tightly behind her back.

He shrugged. 'I don't see why not. You've worked hard this week; you're entitled to some time off. Are you planning on going anywhere special?' His tone was just a little too casual. She had the impression that what he really wanted was for her to account for every minute she intended to spend away from the Hall.

'I'll probably just go home,' she said slightly evasively. 'I'd like to give my mother the painting.'

'Perhaps I should go with you. Then I could give it to her in person.'

His suggestion stunned and shocked her. 'No, you can't do that!' she blurted out. Then, realising he had begun to look at her very keenly, she hurried on, 'I mean, I might not even go there—I haven't made any definite plans——'

Was that suspicion flickering in his eyes? What if it was? she told herself staunchly. What she did in her free time was none of his business. He had no right to try and insinuate his way into her private life.

He seemed to get the message, because he didn't take the suggestion any further, to her utter relief. Anxious to change the subject completely, Alice began to chatter about something else as she put away the last of her clothes.

'You said you saw Tim Dawkins earlier. Did you ask him about that young man who sang at the medieval banquet?'

Dominic frowned. 'No,' he replied curtly. 'Why should I?'

'Oh—I thought you were interested in him.'

'*You* were the one who was interested. He was a competent singer, but as far as I'm concerned, that was as far as it went. I don't even know if we'll use him again.'

'You should,' Alice told him firmly. 'He was more than competent, he really got the audience going and held their attention. Don't you even know his name?'

He shot her an unexpectedly black glance. 'Why this sudden eagerness to find out more about him?'

'There was just something about him. He was—oh, I don't know—so familiar, somehow.'

Dominic prowled away from her, radiating disapproval. 'I've no idea who he is, and I don't *want* to know. Just forget it, Alice.'

'But——'

He swung round and glared at her, and she instantly shut up. She had seen that look on his face before—far too often!—and knew that it would take only one more word on the subject to make him lose his temper all over again.

Why was he so sensitive about it, though? she wondered with a puzzled frown. And who *was* that young man with the dark hair and eyes, who had shot that fierce look straight at Dominic as he had walked out of the Great Hall last night?

Then one obvious explanation hit her with such force that she only just stopped herself from gasping out loud. The strong physical likeness, the same arrogant expression on the hard, well-defined features—it shrieked of some kind of blood-tie. But was it possible? She had thought Dominic was in his early thirties, but he could be older. It was difficult to gauge the age of a man like him with any accuracy. And perhaps the younger man looked more mature than he actually was. If, in fact, he was in his late teens . . . She did some swift mental calculation. Yes, it was just about possible. And it would certainly explain a lot of things. No wonder Dominic Seton was so touchy about the subject of an heir if he already had a grown-up, illegitimate son!

When her whirling head finally cleared a little, she found Dominic had left the room and she was on her own again. Remembering that she had a few precious hours to herself, she grabbed her coat, the painting and her bag, then ran downstairs. All thoughts of Dominic Seton and his problems were pushed to one side for now. She had far more important things on her mind.

It was bitingly cold outside, but her car started first time and the engine ran smoothly. The roads were nearly deserted, and so she made good time, pulling up outside her mother's house by early afternoon.

As her mother opened the door, Alice gave her a happy grin. 'I've been let out of prison for a few hours! Where are they?'

'Wrecking the front room,' answered her mother philosophically. 'Mind you don't get hit by a flying brick as you go in.'

But Alice didn't even hear her. She was already heading in that direction, and her face relaxed into a great smile of pure happiness as she walked through the doorway.

Playing happily on the floor, surrounded by colourful heaps of building bricks, were her twin sons. Paul and James—initially nicknamed Tweedledum and Tweedledee because they were so alike that only she and her mother could tell them apart.

After the hugs and kisses were over, she just sat on the floor with them for a while, watching them while they got on with their game. She never got tired of looking at them, of marvelling at the fact that they were *hers*, the most precious things in her life. And there was absolutely no doubt that she was their mother. They had exactly the same colouring—big, brown eyes fringed with long, dark lashes, and a thick mop of silky, mahogany-brown hair. They had been beautiful babies, now they were strong, healthy toddlers, and one day—although, try as she might, she couldn't quite envisage it—they were going to be handsome men.

'Mummy—play!' ordered James, and Alice gave him a loving poke in his plump tummy, which made him giggle.

'Who are you ordering about, young man?' she demanded with mock sternness. But seconds later she was sprawled out on the floor with them, using the building blocks to make a garage for the small racing cars which James was now pushing round the floor to the accompaniment of a lot of loud 'Vrooms'.

Nowadays, it was difficult for Alice to remember just how horrified and despairing she had been when she had first discovered she was pregnant. Those months when she had carried them had been a nightmare. She had resented every minute of it, had hated the way her body had become so hugely swollen and riddled with endless aches and pains. The birth itself had been long and difficult, and when it was finally over she had been

sure she would hate those babies for ever for all the pain
and misery they had caused her. Then she had seen them
for the first time, and something mysterious and quite
miraculous had happened, something which she had
never expected. A fierce wave of love had rushed over
her, blurring her eyes and actually making her shake.
From that moment on, they had become the centre of
her life. She knew she would work until she dropped in
order to provide for them, would kill if necessary in
order to protect them. Quite simply, she adored them.

It was hard to believe that they were now almost two
years old. Often she resented the time she had to spend
away from them, earning a living, because it meant she
missed so many small but important moments. On the
other hand, she knew she was very lucky in a lot of
ways. Financially, she didn't have too many problems,
now that the agency was doing well, and she had no
worries about finding someone to look after them while
she was working, because her mother was always more
than willing to have them. Since the twins adored their
grandmother, the arrangement worked marvellously
well, and it helped her to feel less guilty about the
number of hours she had to leave them.

She spent the rest of the afternoon making the most
of these precious few hours she had with them. The
three of them played several noisy, boisterous games,
then the twins tucked into their tea, demolishing
everything messily but enthusiastically.

Afterwards, Alice took them up for their bath. As
always, she ended up every bit as wet as they were, and
the twins shrieked with delight as they pelted her with
handfuls of frothy bubbles.

'You're monsters!' she declared lovingly. 'And
hopelessly spoilt.'

'Be a bubble monster,' begged Paul, latching on to

the familiar word.

'Yes, yes!' James egged her on, bouncing up and down with excitement.

Alice poured more bubble bath into the water, whisked it round until fresh froth appeared, and then solemnly scooped handfuls of it on to the top of her head. When it was piled up precariously high, she dabbed more froth on to her eyebrows and added a large blob on the end of her nose; then she sat back on the bath mat and began to pull funny faces at the twins.

It was one of their favourite games at the moment. They would have been quite happy if it had gone on all night. Alice played it for far longer than usual, putting off the moment when the evening would have to come to an end. At last, though, she hauled them out of the bath, hardening her heart against the ritual protest they always put up. She dried them, shovelled them into pyjamas, and then sent them scampering off to bed.

As always, they demanded a story, but she had only been reading for a few minutes when they both fell asleep. They always did everything together, falling asleep at virtually the same time, waking in the same minute, and demanding food simultaneously. She had got used to being confronted with two happy faces, or two slightly tearful ones, as their moods fluctuated together through all the childish emotions, but it still fascinated her. And, as an only child herself, she envied the closeness which the twins already took so much for granted. For the rest of their lives, they would always have someone to turn to, someone they could depend on. And she knew it would be especially important to them, since they didn't have a father. He was dead now—killed in a car crash just over a year ago—but, even if he had still been alive, it wouldn't have made any difference. Right from the start, he had wanted nothing to do with the twins. He had even refused to acknowledge their existence, insisting there was no way he could have been their father.

Alice often worried about what she would tell the twins once they were old enough to start asking questions. Apart from that, though, she never thought about the man who had spent just one night with her and left her with a responsibility that would last a lifetime. The hurt and disillusionment were all a long way behind her now. Although, at the time, she had bitterly regretted what had happened, she knew now that she wouldn't change any of it, if she were to be given the chance.

After the twins had fallen asleep, she stayed in the bedroom for a long while, just gazing at their small, familiar faces. Lying so still, and with their cheeks still faintly flushed from the warm bath, they looked positively angelic. Then she gave a wry grimace. Once they were awake, angelic was just about the last word anyone would use to describe them! The pair of them were always bursting with mischief, but they had loving natures and, as far as she was concerned, they were absolutely perfect.

At last, she reluctantly tiptoed out of the room, leaving just the small night-light burning. Downstairs, she found her mother sitting with her feet propped up on a small stool, blissfully enjoying half an hour's peace and quiet.

'Are you worn out?' asked Alice a little guiltily.

'Yes—and I love it,' replied her mother promptly. 'Do you remember how I used to suffer from insomnia? Not any more! After a day with the twins, I sleep like a log.'

'You're sure it's not too much for you?' Alice persisted anxiously.

'If it were, I'd tell you.' Her mother smiled contentedly. 'I adore being a grandmother—and a well-

used one, at that!' Then her face grew slightly more
serious. 'After your father died, for a long while I felt as
if my own life had ground to a complete halt. Nothing I
did seemed to fill all the long, dreary hours in the day. I
moved house, tried to get interested in redecorating and
refurnishing this place, even joined a couple of local
clubs, but none of it seemed to work. Then one day you
phoned up, told me you were pregnant, and asked if you
could come home for a while.' She grinned ruefully.
'Once I realised I wasn't going to die of shock, I realised
that this was what I'd been needing all along, some kind
of purpose in life. And it's all worked out so incredibly
well, much better than I even expected.'

'I couldn't have carried on working if it hadn't been
for you,' Alice told her with warm gratitude. 'I'd never
have got the agency off the ground.'

'I'm glad it's turning out to be a success. And it's
good for you to keep working, to get out and meet
people. It wouldn't be healthy for either you or the
twins if your whole life centred solely around them.'

'I still feel guilty a lot of the time about leaving them
so much,' Alice admitted.

'Of course you do,' her mother agreed briskly.
'That's only natural. But you're sensible enough to
know that you're not doing them any harm. In fact, it
would be hard to find a couple of happier, more well-
balanced children.'

'Well, a lot of that's due to you—and that reminds
me,' Alice said. 'I've brought you something—a small
present. And I think you're going to like it,' she went on
with a mischievous grin.

She handed over the flat package, then watched her
mother's face as she peeled back the brown paper,
revealing the small painting inside.

For a few moments, her mother went pale and didn't

say anything at all. Then she seemed to recover herself slightly. 'Alice! Is this what I think it is?'

'A genuine Dominic Seton landscape,' Alice said, with some satisfaction. 'Do you like it?'

'But—how did you get it? Why are you giving it to me? Do you have any idea what it's *worth*?' her mother demanded.

'No idea at all,' she admitted cheerfully. 'Except that it's probably quite a lot. As to how I got it—Dominic lost his temper this morning. Giving me the painting was his way of apologising. It was meant for you all along, by the way. I'd already told him you were a fervent admirer of his work.'

'It's marvellous,' enthused her mother, holding up the painting and feasting her eyes on it. 'The man's a genius—I'd love to meet him. What's he like, Alice? Although I adore his work, I know next to nothing about him.'

'He's——' Alice hesitated. How *did* you describe Dominic Seton? 'He's complicated—quick-tempered, sometimes moody—but not vindictive. I don't think he had much of a childhood. He makes light of it, but he must have been very lonely much of the time. And I think he's grown up into a rather solitary adult. Now he's stuck at Rossmore Hall, which he hates, and he rattles around that big house all by himself, which doesn't seem right. He needs——' She stopped, aware that her mother had begun to look at her rather strangely.

'What do you think he needs, Alice?' she prompted quietly.

Alice shook herself briskly. 'I've really no idea. I'm waffling on about something I don't know anything about.' She glanced at her watch, then groaned. 'Is it really that late? I'd better dash. I'll just pop up for a last look at the twins.'

She spent five minutes lingering wistfully by their bedsides, watching them sleep. Then she dropped a light kiss on each smooth forehead, and reluctantly went downstairs to collect her coat, bag and car keys. After a quick goodbye to her mother, she went out to the car and started up the engine.

Many of the narrow country lanes were unlit, forcing her to drive slowly, and it was nearly midnight by the time she arrived back at Rossmore Hall. The familiar dark silhouette loomed on the skyline as she negotiated the last bend in the drive, and her brows drew anxiously together as she saw all the windows were dark. What if there was no one up to let her in?

She was just about to drive round to the rear of the house and try one of the back entrances when she saw the massive front door slowly swing open. Light spilled out from the entrance hall, illuminating the tall figure of the man who stood there, silently waiting for her.

Alice got out of the car and locked it; then she slowly walked towards the house. It was funny, but ever since she had turned in through the gateway, she had had the peculiar sensation of coming home. She knew it was nonsense to feel like that about a place she had spent so little time in, but she still couldn't quite shake off the feeling. And, more disturbing than that, she found the memory of her mother's warm, welcoming house was already beginning to fade. Even the faces of the twins weren't quite as bright in her mind as they had been only minutes ago. How can you forget the twins? she argued fiercely with herself. The answer was that she couldn't, of course she couldn't. Yet her life seemed to be separating into two distinct halves, each half frighteningly unconnected with the other. And, as she reached the entrance to Rossmore Hall and then walked through it, there was no denying that the present was suddenly far

more vivid than even the immediate past. Just the sight of
Dominic Seton's taut face, as he stood there waiting for
her, seemed to have the power to blot out just about
everything else from her mind.

Dominic closed the door behind her; then he just stood
there, so she was forced to turn back to look at him.

'I'm sorry I'm late,' she apologised, a trifle nervously.
'Were you waiting up for me? I suppose you couldn't lock
up until I got here.'

'I was beginning to think that perhaps you weren't
coming back at all,' came his terse reply.

She glanced at him in surprise. 'Why wouldn't I come
back? Anyway, I don't have much choice. I'm under
contract—as you keep reminding me!'

The light in the hall wasn't very bright, and it made his
eyes look almost black.

'And is that the only reason you returned?'

Alice edged away from him fractionally. He seemed in
an odd mood tonight, and it was already beginning to
make her feel jumpy.

'I never walk out on a job when it's only half-way
through,' she retorted. 'At least, not without a very good
reason.'

'Mmm,' he mused softly, almost thoughtfully. 'Then
let's hope you won't consider *this* a very good reason.'

And, before she had time to move or even guess what he
intended doing, he had closed the gap between them and
caught her hard against him. She opened her mouth to
protest, but an instant later it was covered by his own, his
tongue slipping warmly between her lips to prevent her
closing them against him.

The kiss that followed was ruthlessly exploratory, as if
he wanted to record on his memory the touch, taste and
feel of her. Alice was first shocked by this invasive
probing, then her head began to reel a little as it

provoked unexpected responses and small stirrings of pleasure. His hands moved with expert precision, knowing just what they were searching for—and finding it—and her skin began to burn with a radiant heat. Then he withdrew just a fraction, as if satisfied with the results of that first fierce foray, and the kiss slowly turned into something else, a prelude to a much greater pleasure that was just out of reach, but drawing nearer, ever nearer, until it was achingly close; they might even find it with just the touch of their bodies if he would only hold her close enough, tight enough, keep touching her . . .

Instead, though, Dominic let go of her. Alice swayed slightly on her feet, trying to fight her way back to reality but finding it impossibly hard.

'What did you do that for?' she mumbled in a voice that sounded almost drugged.

'Didn't you like it?'

'No. It made me feel——'

'Off balance? Vulnerable?' suggested Dominic softly. 'But that's exactly how I wanted you to feel.' He turned her round and pushed her gently in the direction of the stairs. 'You can go up to bed now, Alice. And I hope you'll find it as difficult to sleep as I will.'

Almost like a zombie, she obeyed him. And, although she did finally manage to get to sleep, she had strange dreams, felt hot and restless, and once muttered his name out loud.

CHAPTER SEVEN

NEXT morning, Alice woke up hoping to find everything had miraculously returned to normal again. It hadn't, though. Some of the strange sensations that had rushed through her last night still seemed to be lingering around and, try as she might, she couldn't get rid of them. She was left with the disturbing impression that her life was dividing into two. One part of her belonged at her mother's house, looking after her twin sons. But the other part seemed to recognise *this* place as home. Rossmore Hall—a house that didn't belong to her, and where she would only be staying for a few more weeks. It didn't make sense.

She took a long, cool shower, hoping it would clear her confused head. When she finally headed downstairs to the library, she did feel slightly more in control of things. She worked hard until the end of the morning, then ate the lunch that Frobisher brought her on a tray.

She spent the afternoon bringing the account books up to date. Then she sat and stared at the pile of outstanding bills. Although the hiring out of the Hall for private functions and banquets was bringing in a steady income, it wasn't making more than a tiny dent in the overall debt. No wonder Dominic was so determined to go through with his scheme for the golf course, combined with a sports and health centre. It certainly needed something fairly drastic to get the estate out of the red.

Deeply lost in thought, thinking about all the

financial problems that Dominic Seton was facing, she
didn't hear him walk quietly into the room. It wasn't
until the two dogs padded in after him, their claws
clicking on the polished wooden floor, that she finally
glanced up.

The instant she saw him, she felt the colour rush into
her face. Damn it! she told herself furiously, I *won't* let
him get to me like this. I don't know what he's doing to
me, but it can just stop!

'You're bright red, and you look as if you'd like to
chuck something straight at me,' Dominic remarked,
with a touch of amusement. 'Have I done anything to
particularly upset you?'

'You know perfectly well what you did,' she muttered
resentfully.

He settled himself easily into a chair. One of the dogs
immediately came over and rested its head adoringly on
his knee. Alice switched her gaze from Dominic and
glared at the wolfhound instead. Why couldn't the
stupid animal see him for what he really was? If the dog
had an ounce of sense in its dumb head, it would be
biting his ankle!

'Is this bout of bad temper because of last night?'
Dominic enquired casually. 'That one little kiss?'

Alice's eyebrows instantly shot up. The way she
remembered it, it had been more than just 'one little
kiss'. Her skin began to burn again at the very thought
of it, and she hurriedly pushed the disturbing memories
out of her mind. She wanted to be very cool and
controlled this afternoon, and she wasn't going to
manage that unless she could forget all about the hard,
yet sweet, touch of his lips.

'You brought me here to work,' she got out at last,
relieved to find her voice sounded fairly steady.
'Anything—else—wasn't included in the contract.'

'And you think we ought to stick more closely to the agreement we made?'

'Yes,' she said very firmly.

'That sounds reasonable to me,' he agreed.

Alice looked at him suspiciously. She had the unsettling feeling that he was just playing games with her; that inwardly he was laughing at her awkwardness, and enjoying the uncertainty that was starting to sweep over her more and more whenever he was around.

'If things don't improve, I might have to—to terminate our contract,' she blurted out.

'And take the consequences?' A note of warning suddenly sounded in his voice.

'Yes,' she said defiantly. Then her resistance crumbled a fraction. 'I don't know why you're so determined to keep me here,' she mumbled.

Dominic's gaze rested on her with level intensity, making her shake inwardly.

'Don't you, Alice?' he challenged softly.

She stared back at him edgily. 'What do you want from me?'

'Everything I can get. There are so many things in this life I can't have. When I find something I *can* have—and something which I want very much—then I keep going after it until I finally get it.'

His cool declaration shook her to her roots.

'That's a pretty lousy attitude to adopt!' she said hotly. 'It means that you always put what you want first, that you don't give a damn about other people's needs or feelings.'

He took her accusation quite calmly, which unsettled her even further. An outburst of temper would have been easier to deal with.

'I don't believe in making anyone do anything against their will,' Dominic said at last. Ignoring her snort

of disbelief, he went on, 'I made you sign a legal
contract, which imposed certain penalties on you if you
walked out before your job here was finished. I don't
think there was anything particularly unfair about that.
As for anything else that's happened between us—that
wasn't covered by the contract, Alice,' he said softly.
'There isn't a legal document in the world that could
force you to touch me, to kiss me. You were free at any
time to run away—if you wanted to.'

His last words hung heavily in the air, and she deeply
resented their implication. He made it sound as if she
had been actively chasing after him, and it hadn't been
like that at all!

'That night after—after the medieval banquet,' she
spluttered. 'You followed me to my room, followed me
right into my *bed*. But it certainly wasn't at my
invitation.'

'But you went along with it,' he reminded her
relentlessly. 'You even enjoyed it, until you suddenly
got scared. And when you wanted me to stop, I
did—even though it was the very last thing on earth I
wanted to do by then,' he went on in a slightly harsh
tone. 'So don't ever accuse me of making you do
something against your will, Alice. I might have
resorted to gentle persuasion, but it never went any
further than that.'

Small inner tremors shook her all over again as she
remembered just what forms that 'gentle persuasion'
had taken. Then she ruthlessly pulled herself together.
She was not going to let this man get to her with his
clever words—and his clever hands. There was nothing
to be afraid of if she just remained cool, and hung on to
her own self-control.

She already knew that it wasn't Dominic Seton
himself that made her so very nervous. Always strictly

honest with herself, Alice now freely admitted what she had instinctively known all along. It was her own reaction to this man that was making her so edgy and uncertain. It had been such a long time since she had responded so positively to any male. She had thought it was safely buried for ever, that side of her nature which, ever since the twins' conception, she had thought of as a shameful—and dangerous—weakness. Now that passionate response was springing to life again, filling her veins with warm longing and making her ache emptily inside. She wished it would just go away again, and leave her in peace. She didn't want to feel like this, and not knowing what to do about it, how to stop it, made her feel even more helpless and vulnerable.

'So where do you suggest we should go from here?' she asked in a low voice, at last.

'Right now, I'd like you to come up to the studio and sit for me for a couple of hours,' Dominic answered easily. 'The light's particularly good this afternoon.'

Her head shot up in surprise. It definitely wasn't the reply she had been expecting, and it briefly threw her off balance. 'Oh, I don't think—I've still got quite a lot of work to do——' she began in a flustered voice.

'Leave it until tomorrow.' His tone was firm, and brooked no further argument. He got up and walked towards the door, and she automatically began to follow him. Then she suddenly stopped. She didn't *have* to do everything this man ordered.

Dominic turned his head, suddenly seeming to realise that she wasn't directly behind him. 'Come on, Alice,' he said peremptorily, 'I want to get some more sketches done before the light begins to fade.'

Her legs obediently began to move again, and Alice gave up the unequal struggle to resist him. When he called, she followed—it was as simple as that. She just hoped he didn't realise how much influence he had over her, because then she really would be in serious trouble.

Upstairs in the studio, she settled into the chair she had sat in before. The two wolfhounds stretched out at her feet, and the next half-hour was surprisingly peaceful, as Dominic did half a dozen leisurely sketches.

Since Alice didn't have much choice except to look at him, she had more time than she wanted to study every small detail of his face. She already knew the strong, dark planes far too well, but now there was a chance to linger over the finer details: the line of his mouth, the underlying bone structure, the tiny marks of temper lurking warningly in the corners of his eyes, the smooth skin that still held traces of a tan that she supposed had been acquired at his home in Provence.

And after a while she noticed something else, which rather surprised her. 'You look so relaxed while you're working,' she told him.

Dominic glanced up. 'Why not? I'm doing something that I enjoy more than anything else.' His eyes briefly gleamed. '*Almost* more than anything else.' Then he looked at her in amusement. 'Alice, are you blushing again?'

'Of course not!' she said with some annoyance. 'I'm just a bit hot, that's all.'

'And I always thought it was rather chilly in this studio,' he mocked her lightly.

'Do you want me to sit here much longer?' she asked stiffly, ignoring that last gentle gibe.

'Just a few more minutes. I'll finish this sketch and then we'll call it a day. The light's beginning to go now, anyway.'

His pencil skimmed over the paper with total

sureness, and Alice watched in reluctant admiration. She had seen some of the sketches he had done the other day, and she had been amazed that he could capture so much with just a few spare lines. Her mother had declared that Dominic Seton was a genius and, although Alice was painfully ignorant when it came to art, even she could see he had an exceptional talent.

Dominic finally put down his pencil; then he just sat looking at her for a couple of minutes.

Alice fidgeted uncomfortably. 'Is that it?' she said at last, anxious to escape from the scrutiny of those fierce, dark eyes.

'You've got beautiful skin,' he said musingly, as if she hadn't even spoken. 'Pale, but definitely not colourless. It's going to be difficult to get the tones exactly right.'

'Well, that's your problem, not mine. Can I go now?'

'I suppose you wouldn't pose nude for me?' he asked casually, totally ignoring her request.

'No!' It came out as a nervous squeak, and so she tried again. 'No,' she repeated, much more firmly.

He didn't seem either angry or surprised by her refusal. 'Any particular reason why you won't do it?'

'I'd have thought that was pretty obvious!'

'Not to me.'

'Well—when the painting was finished, it would hang in an exhibition somewhere. Right?'

'It's more than likely,' Dominic agreed.

'And hundreds—thousands—of people would come in and stare at it. Stare at *me*—without any clothes on——'

As her voice trailed away, Dominic nodded. 'I see. So your main objection to being painted in the nude is that crowds of people would see it, and know what you looked like naked?'

'Yes. Isn't that enough?' she demanded indignantly.

'It's certainly understandable. But it sounds as if you don't actually object to posing nude. Only to people seeing the finished painting.'

'I didn't say that!'

'Yes, you did,' he told her calmly. 'And I think you were telling the truth. After you'd got over your initial embarrassment—and every life model experiences that the first few times—I think you'd feel perfectly relaxed and happy posing for me, Alice.'

'I would not,' she denied vehemently. 'Anyway, you don't paint nudes.'

'Not very often,' he agreed. 'But it's rare to find someone like you, who'd make such an exceptional model. Will you at least think about it?'

'I don't need to,' she retorted. 'I shan't change my mind. It's a head and shoulders portrait, or nothing at all.'

'Stubborn as well as prudish?' he mocked lightly.

Alice got angrily to her feet. 'Just because I won't take my clothes off for you——'

His own face instantly darkened. There was no trace of amusement on his features now, and Alice flinched nervously as one of those abrupt changes of mood swept over him yet again. 'Do you think that's why I asked you?' he demanded. 'So I could enjoy some cheap peep-show?' He strode swiftly over to her, and an instant later his hands were tightly gripping her shoulders. 'This is my *work*,' he told her tersely, gesturing briefly at the studio. 'And it's damned hard work at times. It's how I made my living most of my adult life, until Rossmore Hall was wrapped around my neck, like some bloody great albatross. And I don't mix work and play. From the moment you walk through that studio door, you're perfectly safe. I don't make a point of jumping on my models before the paint's even dry!'

He let go of her again, walked rapidly out of the studio, and then slammed the door angrily behind him. Alice blinked miserably. She always seemed to say the wrong thing, to misunderstand his motives entirely. Then she shook her head with a sudden rush of impatience. It wasn't something that she should even be worrying about. If she and Dominic Seton didn't understand each other, what did it matter? The world wouldn't come to an end because of it!

The next morning, Dominic left early for London. He had business meetings there that were going to occupy him all day, and Alice was relieved about that. It meant that she could relax for a few hours and get on with her work without any interruptions.

Early in the afternoon, Frobisher came into the library. 'There's a young man to see Lord Rossmore,' he told her. 'Perhaps you could deal with him?'

'Do you know what he wants?' asked Alice.

Frobisher gave a faint but audible sniff. 'I didn't ask him,' he replied. From that, Alice deduced that he didn't consider it part of his duties to deal with the problems of casual visitors to the house.

'You'd better bring him in here,' she said. 'I'll see if I can help him.'

A couple of minutes later, a young man strode into the library. Alice's eyes opened very wide as she immediately recognised him. His face, like Dominic's, would be hard to forget, with its dark gaze, impatient expression and unconscious arrogance.

'Hello,' she greeted him, giving a warm smile. 'I've seen you before—you sang at the medieval banquet. You were very good.'

'I've come to see Lord Rossmore,' the young man said abruptly. 'Is he here?'

Alice's friendly smile faded away. So the resemblance to Dominic was more than physical!

'He's gone to London,' she told him, rather more coolly. 'I'm afraid he won't be back until late this evening. Can I help you at all?'

'No,' he said curtly. Then he seemed to realise he wasn't being very polite. 'Sorry,' he added briefly, 'I didn't mean to be rude. Perhaps you could give this to Lord Rossmore when he returns.'

He placed a thin folder on the desk, and Alice looked at it curiously. 'What is it?'

'It's a petition.' The young man shrugged. 'I told everyone that it wouldn't do the slightest bit of good, but they wanted to go ahead with it, so here it is.'

'A petition?' she repeated, with a faint frown. 'Against what?'

He looked at her with a touch of impatience. 'I'd have thought that was fairly obvious. Against the proposed golf course and sports centre, of course.' An expression of disgust briefly crossed his face. 'A few names on a list isn't going to persuade Lord Rossmore to change his mind, but some people around here still think they can make him see reason, that he's open to persuasion.'

Alice gazed back at him steadily. 'Perhaps you think it's more effective to smash windows and damage cars?' she suggested, remembering the recent spate of petty vandalism.

The young man's face instantly darkened, and the resemblance to Dominic became even more startling. 'I'm not that stupid!' he retorted angrily. 'What good does it do to go around causing deliberate damage? As soon as I found out what was happening, I put a stop to it.' He stared at her challengingly. 'You haven't had any more incidents during the last few days, have you?'

'No, we haven't,' she agreed. Then she studied him with fresh interest. 'You seem to have quite a lot of influence around here.'

'But not with the people who count,' he growled frustratedly.

'And that's why you wanted to see Lord Rossmore? To try and persuade him in person?'

'I don't know why I even bothered. He's not the sort of man who'll listen to reason. And he certainly doesn't give a damn about the house or the estate. He just wants to use it to generate high profits, so he can live in luxury on the proceeds!'

Alice immediately shook her head. 'If you think that, you obviously don't know him very well. And you don't understand the very real problems he's facing.'

'How *can* we understand, when he won't even discuss them with us?' The young man gestured towards the petition. 'Just give it to him, will you? Then at least I'll have kept my promise to deliver it.'

As he turned round and began to leave, Alice called after him. 'You haven't told me your name.'

He glanced back at her in surprise. 'It isn't important. But if you really want to know, it's Toby. Toby Collins.'

With that, he left the library, and Alice stared after him, rather shaken by the unexpected encounter. She remembered all her earlier suspicions, and wondered if they could possibly be right. Was this tall, dark young man Dominic Seton's son?

Even if he is, it's none of your business, she reminded herself sharply. With an effort, she forced herself to get back to the work in front of her. All the same, she felt completely unsettled for the rest of the day, and, when Frobisher brought her tea, she found her appetite seemed to have deserted her.

She spent the evening in one of the smaller drawing-rooms. Because the weather was still very cold, a fire had been lit to supplement the central heating, and the flames added an extra cosiness to the room. There was a television set tucked away in the corner, and Alice watched it for a while, but couldn't find any programme that held her interest for more than a few minutes. Finally, she turned it off and picked up a book, but she kept losing the thread of the story as her mind wandered off in other directions.

At eleven o'clock, she finally tossed the book to one side and decided to take herself off to bed. She wasn't particularly tired, but perhaps she would manage to fall asleep after a relaxing soak in a warm bath.

Then she heard the sound of a car pulling up on the gravel drive in front of the Hall. Tweaking the heavy curtains back just a couple of inches, she peered out and saw Dominic getting out of the car. Snow was beginning to fall again, and there was already a light layer settling on the ground. Dominic began to walk towards the front entrance, and she hurriedly let the curtain fall back into place again.

He would probably go straight upstairs, she decided. He had had a long day; he no doubt wanted a shower and then several hours' sleep. She would wait here until he had gone to his room, and then go up herself.

Only it didn't work out that way. A couple of minutes later, the door to the drawing-room opened and Dominic came in, looking tired and frozen.

'Frobisher said he'd lit a fire in here,' he said. 'God, I'm cold! The damned heater in the car wasn't working properly.'

He poured himself a whisky, then sprawled on the sofa in front of the fire. 'Are you coming or going?' he asked slightly irritably as she hovered uncertainly near the doorway.

'Er—I was going,' she said.

'Stay for a few minutes,' he instructed. 'Bring me up to date on what's been happening during the day.'

Alice settled herself down on the far end of the sofa, as far away from him as she could get without making the whole thing look too obvious.

'It's been fairly quiet,' she told him. 'There are a few letters for you to sign in the morning, but nothing particularly urgent. And I've had a couple of enquiries about provisional bookings for the Great Hall. One's from an American company—they want to hold their annual dinner here. There'll be a minimum of a hundred and fifty people, and cost doesn't seem to be any problem.'

'Mmm.' He didn't seem very interested; in fact, he had closed his eyes now. She had the impression that he was already half asleep. She was just wondering if she could creep out without disturbing him, when she remembered the visit from Toby Collins. Sooner or later, Dominic was going to have to be told about it, and she decided she might as well get it over now, and be done with it.

'You remember the young man who sang at the banquet?' she began, a trifle nervously. 'He came to see me today. Or rather, he came to see you, but you weren't here,' she went on, watching Dominic very carefully as she tried to gauge his reaction.

His eyes had flickered open again now, and his mouth had set into a distinctly forbidding line.

'What did he want?'

'To hand in a petition.' Alice quickly explained what had happened, her voice quavering a fraction as she saw the ominous dark expression settling over his face.

'In other words, they're trying to tell me what I can

or cannot do with my own land!'

'Of course not,' she said placatingly. 'They just want you to—well, to think again, perhaps try and find another alternative. One that isn't so drastic, and won't affect everyone around here quite so much.'

'There *is* another alternative,' Dominic growled. 'It's called bankruptcy. The tours and banquets aren't enough. Not even the sale of all my paintings would save the place. But perhaps that wouldn't worry them too much. I'm not exactly popular around here. No one's going to shed any tears if I lose my house, my entire estate.'

'That's nonsense. No one wants you to lose anything. Anyway,' she went on, her brows coming together thoughtfully, 'you're suddenly getting very possessive over your inheritance, aren't you? My land, my house, my estate——' she quoted back at him. 'Are you starting to change your mind about not wanting any of it?'

It was some time before he finally answered her. 'Things can get into your blood without you even realising it's happening,' he muttered at last. 'Setons have lived here for hundreds of years—and I *am* a Seton.' He glanced broodily around the room. 'These last few months—it's the longest stretch of time I've ever spent here, apart from when I was very young. I suppose it's the first chance I've had to get to know it, to realise that it actually is my home.'

'You said you felt trapped here,' she reminded him.

'Yes, I know. And sometimes I still do. But just recently, I've begun to feel——'

'Feel what?' Alice prompted gently.

Unexpectedly, his mouth relaxed into a wry grin. 'That perhaps I could spend the rest of my life here without becoming completely suicidal.'

Alice's eyebrows shot up. 'I never thought I'd hear you say that.'

'Nor did I. Perhaps I wouldn't even be admitting it now if it wasn't late at night and I wasn't dog-tired.' He stifled a yawn. 'Why are you sitting so far away from me, Alice?'

His unexpected question sent a tiny quiver through her nerve-ends.

'Am I?' she parried guardedly.

A gleam of amusement lit his eyes. 'I like these games that we play together,' he told her softly.

'I'm not playing games,' Alice replied in a stiff voice. 'You might think that sort of thing's fun, but I definitely don't.'

'Oh, no, I forgot,' he agreed, his dark gaze still dancing. 'You like to pretend to be prudish at times.'

She instantly got to her feet. 'It isn't a pretence!'

'Then I only imagined that we had such an enjoyable—and *uninhibited*—time in bed together a few nights ago?' he mocked her gently.

Alice coloured furiously. 'Nothing actually happened! And anyway, it didn't count, I'd had too much wine. That's why I——'

'Why you were so deliciously abandoned?' Dominic finished for her. 'You only behave like that when you're drunk?'

But Alice didn't answer. She didn't even want to think about the way she behaved when she wasn't entirely sober.

Dominic got to his feet; then he casually moved towards her. Alice instantly backed away, her pulses suddenly beginning to thunder at top speed.

'Still scared of me?' he challenged.

She nearly said 'yes', wanting desperately to give into the impulse to turn and flee. A small spark of pride wouldn't let her, though. Instead, she lifted her head defiantly and didn't back away any further.

'Certainly not. But it's late. I think I'll go up to my room now.'

'But I want you to stay here—with me.' He didn't even give her a chance to refuse. Before she could get out a single word, he slid his hand through hers and pulled her down beside him on to the sofa. 'Talk to me,' he invited.

'About what?' she responded nervously.

'Anything you like. Tell me more about yourself—that's an easy enough subject to start with.'

'No,' she said at once, 'it's—it's boring.'

'I wouldn't be bored,' he assured her. 'There are so many things I'd like to know about you, Alice.'

'Such as what?' she queried warily.

Dominic's fingers were still lightly closed around her own, their grip just firm enough to stop her pulling away from him and escaping.

'For a start, I'd be interested to hear why you suddenly got so scared that night we went to bed together.'

'We did *not* go to bed,' Alice insisted furiously. 'Don't keep saying we did. It makes it sound as if——'

'As if we're lovers?' enquired Dominic in a lazy voice. Then he grinned. 'And now you're blushing again. You really are an old-fashioned girl. But you still haven't answered my question,' he reminded her.

'I don't know why you're in the least interested,' she muttered edgily.

'I'd have thought that was fairly obvious. I don't want the same thing to happen again.'

Alice swallowed hard. 'Well, that's easy to arrange. Just stay away from me and everything will be fine.'

His eyes were glittering again, but not with amusement this time. 'But I don't want to stay away from you,' he told her huskily. 'And I don't think it's what you want either, Alice.'

'You're an expert on what I want?' she retorted.

'Not yet. But I'd like to be.'

The velvet tones of his voice seemed to be lethally undermining her resistance. And she hadn't even had anything to drink tonight, so she couldn't blame it on that.

'I wish you'd stop doing this to me,' she whispered unhappily.

'Doing what?'

'Forcing me into a situation that I don't want to be in.'

The grip of his hand lightened still further, so that only his fingertips were gently resting against her skin. 'I'm not holding you a prisoner. You can run away—if you want to.'

Yet she couldn't, although she didn't know why. She was pinned to the sofa by the same irresistible force that had kept her pinned to the bed on the night he had followed her to her room. She didn't know what it was, she couldn't put a name to it, but it was definitely there, like an invisible chain that was binding her to him.

She could sense Dominic's pleasure at her helplessness. He was a man who liked to get what he wanted—and what he wanted right now was her.

Alice, don't let this happen, she warned herself shakily. Remember what it leads to, don't ever be stupid enough to go through that kind of hell all over again . . .

But reason was already drifting away as Dominic bent his head slightly and found the warm skin at the nape of her neck.

'Mmm,' he murmured appreciatively. 'You taste delicious.'

His voice was as seductive as his touch, the low timbre finding a familiar, responsive chord somewhere deep inside her. Then the hot weakness began to spread through her, stirring up small surges of pleasure, mixed with panic.

Damn! she thought a little wildly. Why can't I be frigid? Why do I have to have a body that leaps into life at just a touch, starts wanting all the things it shouldn't have?

She gritted her teeth as Dominic's hands began expertly searching out the warm, soft places that it gave him intense pleasure to touch. Her own nerve-ends instantly leapt in response, flooding her with warm delight, and she closed her eyes in despair.

All right, she told herself weakly. You can have five minutes. Just five minutes of these frighteningly addictive sensations. That should be enough to satisfy you, enough to stave off the worst of this longing.

Dominic seemed to know the very instant she voluntarily lowered her resistance. A small grunt of satisfaction sounded in his throat, and his hands became slower, more patient, as if he knew he had plenty of time in which to accomplish all that he intended.

He removed her jumper, then began to unbutton the blouse which she was wearing underneath for extra warmth. Uneasily, Alice stirred. She didn't want this to go too far. She wasn't naïve, she knew how unfair it would be to him.

'I don't want——' she began unsteadily.

'Never mind for now what you want or don't want,' Dominic instructed firmly.

But Alice was determined that he should understand what she was trying to say. 'You ought to stop now. If you don't, you'll be——'

'Frustrated?' he finished for her drily, as she fumbled

for the right words. 'Quite possibly. But that'll be my problem, not yours.' The blouse parted under his hands, leaving the swell of her breasts very visible above the low line of her bra. 'Beautiful,' came his husky verdict as his dark gaze lingered on them. Expertly, he slid one arm under her legs and levered them up, so she found herself lying on the sofa beside him. He tucked a cushion under her head. 'Comfortable?'

Dazedly, she nodded. Then his fingers began to explore the warmth of one breast, easing their way gently under the thin material of the bra and then resting there contentedly.

Alice drew in a ragged breath. 'Dominic, I won't make love with you,' she told him bluntly.

He didn't seem angry, and he didn't try to argue with her. 'Maybe. And maybe not,' he said in a relaxed voice. 'It's not something that you even have to think about right now. You can decide when the time comes.'

Before she could tell him there was absolutely no chance of her changing her mind, his mouth closed over hers in a kiss that left her head whirling, so she couldn't even remember what she had been going to say that had seemed of such importance. At the same time, her hands instinctively closed over him, sliding under his leather jacket, savouring the strength of the muscles under the fine cotton of his shirt.

All sense of reality started to slip away from her; try as she might, she couldn't hold on to it. It was a familiar sensation, and yet at the same time there *was* something new about it, because it hadn't been quite like this before. Last time this had happened to her, her head had been spinning from too much alcohol. This time she was stone-cold sober, and somehow that was making it even more intense, more pleasurable—more irresistible.

Dominic's fingers brushed and caressed, his mouth

lightly nibbled, and her body began to melt with hot longing. He moved nearer, adding the heat of his own body to the warmth that pulsed through her, and she stared dazedly up at his dark, familiar face. He looked straight back at her with a fierce, yet unexpectedly tender, look in his eyes.

'I like touching you,' he told her huskily, his hands shifting over her slowly and sensually, as if to emphasise his words. 'But I like being touched in return.'

Alice's own hands moved at once in involuntary response. He was still fully dressed, and yet that didn't seem to make the slightest difference. Although there was the rough rasp of material under her sensitive fingertips, all she was aware of was the hard, vital body underneath, shifting a little restlessly now, as she unashamedly explored every vibrant inch of him.

'Enough!' Dominic finally instructed, his breath abruptly catching in his throat. He caught hold of her wrist and held it a prisoner, stopping her from inflicting any more of those killingly pleasurable caresses on him. For a few moments, he kept very still. Then his breathing steadied a fraction, and his mouth relaxed into a rueful smile. 'You always manage to surprise me, Alice,' he went on, shaking his head rather wryly. 'Just when I'm expecting you to pull your usual prudish act, you turn round and practically seduce me! Not that I don't like it,' he added with a grin. 'I do. But you told me earlier you didn't want me to make love to you. Does that decision still hold? If it does, you'd better tell me right now. Another few minutes of this, and I might not be willing to listen to you.'

But she couldn't think straight; she had hardly even heard what he had said. More and more, he was beginning to have this effect on her. He spoke to her, touched her, and she forgot all about her fears, her self-imposed inhibitions, her responsibilities. It was scary, and

yet somehow marvellous to feel like this; she wanted to
hold on to the soaring sense of freedom for a few more
moments, just a few more moments . . .

Dominic was staring at her intently, as if trying to figure
out what was going on inside her head. Then he gave a
brief shrug, as if he had given up on the puzzle. 'All right,'
he said softly, 'if you don't want to talk, that's fine by me.
I've got other things on my mind right now—and I don't
think they'll wait for very much longer——'

This time, the quality of his lovemaking was very
different. There were no more light, almost teasing
caresses, no more gentle games played with lips and
tongue. Every movement was hard and sure now,
exquisitely pleasurable but forceful, and all leading
relentlessly towards one ultimate conclusion.

Shocked out of the dreamy reverie that she had been
floating in so warmly and comfortably, Alice gave a small
gasp. What was he doing? Then she tossed her head from
side to side as Dominic ruthlessly subjected her breasts to a
sweetly savage onslaught. For a few moments, she was
caught and entangled in the storm of pleasure he was
whipping up, drifting helplessly as her muscles jumped and
contracted out of control, racked by spasms of aching
need. Then her head cleared for an instant, she realised
what was happening, and she let out a small moan of
dismay and fear.

'No!'

'*Yes*, Alice,' Dominic told her thickly. 'I gave you the
chance to back out—you didn't take it——' He fitted
himself against her so that she had the whirling impression
that she was already part of that deeply aroused body.
'Tell me that you don't want me,' he challenged in a husky
tone. 'And don't lie to me. I'll know if you lie.'

Oh, God, what could she do? She *did* want him. This
man had somehow torn right through all her defences;

she would have given just about anything for a few
carefree, wonderful hours in his arms. He stirred all her
emotions, she ached for the intimate touch of him.

Yet even that wasn't quite enough to exorcise the
underlying fear that had suddenly forced its way to the
surface.

'I'm frightened,' she blurted out shakenly.

Dominic stared at her incredulously. 'Of what? Not of
me,' he said with utter certainty.

Alice shivered. She would have to tell him. It was only
fair, after letting things get so far that they had nearly
rocketed beyond the control of either of them.

She averted her eyes so she wouldn't have to look at
him.

'Of getting pregnant,' she muttered.

What would he do? she wondered edgily. Airily dismiss
her fears? Tell her he would take care of things, so it
couldn't possibly happen? Only she wouldn't swallow that
line again. Oh, yes, men certainly took care of things!
They arranged it so they got precisely what they wanted,
and to hell with any consequences.

She let her gaze slide back to Dominic, nervous now as
she waited for his reaction. As her eyes fixed on his face,
though, a spasm of shock ran through her. He looked as if
she had just hit him!

An instant later, he physically withdrew from her. All
trace of desire had abruptly disappeared from his face,
which had taken on a dark and brooding quality. For the
first time since she had known him, he scared her a little,
and she stared at him with a rush of apprehension.

'What is it?'

'What is it?' he repeated harshly. He met her gaze
steadily, and Alice was alarmed to find that he looked
almost like a stranger. 'Let me tell you exactly what it is.
It's a rather macabre joke.'

'I don't understand,' she whispered.

Dominic swung himself to his feet. 'Of course you don't. But that's because I've never told you a very personal piece of information about myself. There's no chance that I'd have made you—or anyone else—pregnant.' Seeing the bewildered expression that spread across her face, he gave a grim, totally humourless smile. 'Do you want to know the medical term for it? Sterile. You'd have been quite safe with me, Alice. Tonight—and every other night, for the rest of my damned life!'

She couldn't say a word, but it didn't matter. He had already walked swiftly out of the room, leaving her in the empty silence, every inch of her quietly vibrating with the intense shock of his announcement.

CHAPTER EIGHT

THERE was no sleep for Alice that night. Next morning, she was heavy-eyed, and had a thumping headache caused by tension. She spent ages getting showered and dressed and, even when she was finally ready, she lingered in her room for a few extra minutes. Although she was ashamed to admit it, even to herself, she was putting off the moment when she would have to come face to face with Dominic. She didn't know what to say to him. Or perhaps she was simply afraid of saying too much. She didn't know how to handle what was beginning to happen between them.

Since it couldn't be put off indefinitely, she finally ventured downstairs. Frobisher had set two places at the breakfast table, but there was no sign of Dominic. Either he was still in bed—which Alice thought unlikely—or he had got up very early and gone out. He was probably as reluctant to see her as she was to see him, she decided. Last night, he had told her something that few people in this world—if anyone—could know about. No doubt he was already deeply regretting that abrupt confession. But, since he could hardly take it back, he was probably doing the next best thing, and avoiding her.

Leaving most of her breakfast untouched, she got up and made her way to the library. She couldn't concentrate on work, though, and an hour later she sat back and stared blankly ahead of her.

She needed to go home. If she spent some time with

the twins, perhaps it would help to get her life back into perspective again. She needed to cuddle them, play with them, scold them, do all the things that helped to make up the normal pattern of her life. Maybe then she could start to forget about Dominic Seton. It shouldn't be too difficult, she told herself stubbornly. Right now, she felt desperately sorry for him—she was ready to admit that. It must be pretty grim, rattling around this great house on his own, and having to live with the knowledge that he could never have a family of his own to fill the echoingly empty rooms with laughter and childish chatter. If she let herself think about it too much, she would probably start to feel an aching sense of pity for him. But she wasn't going to let herself do that. She couldn't afford to. Her own life was already too full of obstacles and difficulties. She needed all her strength to overcome them and make a good life for herself and the twins. They were her first—her only—responsibility, and she had better not forget that.

She went upstairs and fetched her coat, her bag and her car keys. Then she quietly left the house, got into the car and started up the engine. As she drove away, she couldn't resist a quick glance back over her shoulder. Under its light covering of snow, Rossmore Hall looked like something out of a dream. She was ready to admit now that she wasn't at all sure she would be coming back here again. She certainly hadn't forgotten that contract Dominic had made her sign, but she didn't think he would hold her to it, not after last night.

She reached the end of the drive, and turned on to the narrow country road. The thin layer of snow had made it slippery, and she concentrated on her driving, glad to have something positive she could focus her thoughts on. There was a sharp bend in the road just ahead, and she slowed almost to a halt, knowing she would have to take it carefully under these icy conditions. She eased the car round the tight curve, then let out an involuntary gasp. Someone hadn't been so cautious—their car was slewed right across the road, the bonnet buried in the thick hedge on the far side.

Alice managed to stop without actually hitting the other car. Then she recognised it, and her heart suddenly began thundering away at a crazy speed. A split second later, she was scrambling out and rushing over to it.

Wrenching open the door, she bent her head so she could see inside. 'Dominic? Dominic!'

He was slumped over the wheel, and didn't seem to respond to the sound of her voice. With a sinking feeling in the pit of her stomach, she realised he wasn't wearing his safety-belt.

'Idiot!' she half sobbed under her breath, and went to lift his head up, but then stopped. She didn't know what injuries he had. She could do him real harm if she tried to move him. Anyway, there was no way she could get him out of the car on her own. He would be an absolute dead weight.

Trembling violently, she stepped back and then stared despairingly up the road in both directions. Not a soul in sight! What on earth was she going to do?

Then Dominic gave a faint moan, and she dived back in the car again.

'Are you all right?' she asked anxiously. 'Dominic, say something, *please*.'

He managed to raise his head, but it was pretty obvious he didn't know where he was or what had happened. Blood was trickling down his face from a gash on his forehead, and one hand seemed to be holding his ribs, as if instinctively seeking out the place that was giving him the most pain.

Torn between the instinct to stay right here with him and the knowledge that she ought to go and fetch help, Alice glanced frantically along the road again. Then she gave a gulp of pure relief as she saw a figure in the distance.

'Hey!' She waved her arms, then yelled again. Whoever it was, he was riding a bicycle, skimming confidently over the frozen ground. Then he drew nearer, and Alice suddenly recognised the dark young face. Toby Collins—for a moment she felt a spurt of apprehension. It would have been much easier if it had been someone else who had come rushing to the rescue. Then she pushed all her misgivings to one side. They weren't important. All that mattered was getting Dominic back to the house.

Toby got off his bike and swiftly came over. Then his face settled into a disapproving frown as he saw the slumped occupant of the car.

'I suppose the damned fool took the bend too fast!'

'That doesn't matter right now. You've got to help him.' When Toby still hesitated, Alice seized hold of his arm. 'You've *got* to.'

'He won't appreciate it,' Toby warned.

'Perhaps not. But I will.'

Toby shot a piercing glance at her, which was unnervingly like Dominic's in its ability to suddenly perceive the meaning behind her words.

'All right, then. Let's take a look at him.' He slid into the seat beside Dominic, studied the cut on his forehead, and then ran his fingers lightly over the rest of him. 'I don't think there's anything broken,' he pronounced at last.

'You're sure of that?' Alice asked anxiously.

'Of course not. I'm no expert. But I think he'd be making a lot more fuss if he'd actually fractured something.'

'If you think Dominic would make a fuss over a broken bone, you don't know him very well,' Alice said wryly. Then her brow became furrowed again. 'Can we get him into my car? Then I can drive him back to the house. He ought to see a doctor.'

'It would be far easier if we just shifted him into the passenger seat,' replied Toby. 'Then I can drive him back in this car, and you can follow along behind.'

With some half-hearted co-operation from the semi-conscious Dominic, they managed to shove him over so that Toby could slide behind the wheel. Expertly, he backed the car out of the hedge and straightened it up; then he gave Alice the thumbs-up sign. 'There's nothing wrong with it, except a few dents and scratches on the bodywork. See you back at the Hall.'

Alice rushed over to her own car, then roared off after them. By the time she reached the Hall, Toby had brought the other car to a halt in front of the main entrance. She jumped out and ran over, only to find that Dominic had made a remarkably rapid recovery during the short journey. His eyes were fully open now, although still not quite in focus, and he was obviously aware of what was going on.

'How do you feel?' Alice questioned him worriedly.

'I'll be fine once I get inside,' Dominic growled. He went to get out of the car, but he had obviously over-estimated his rate of recovery. As his legs buckled, he gave a dark scowl of frustration.

Toby looked at him coolly. 'It looks as if you can either accept a helping hand, or stay right there.'

Dominic's face grew even blacker, but he had enough sense to admit that Toby was right. After a long pause, he curtly nodded, and reached out a hand to the younger man.

There was a rather curious expression on Toby's face as he took it. Then he put Dominic's arm around his shoulder, hauled him to his feet, and took much of his weight as the two of them slowly made their way into the house.

With Dominic at last safely deposited in a comfortable chair in the drawing-room, Alice let out a sigh of relief. 'I'll go and phone the doctor.'

'I don't need a doctor,' Dominic cut in at once. 'I've just got a few bruises, that's all.'

'And a gash on the head,' Toby reminded him. 'That'll probably need a couple of stitches.' He turned to Alice. 'Ring for the doctor,' he instructed.

Dominic glared at him. 'You seem to be taking a lot on yourself!'

Toby returned his gaze steadily, obviously not in the least overawed by Dominic's forceful presence. 'I suppose I am,' he agreed calmly. 'Are you telling me I don't have the right?'

To her astonishment, Dominic was the first one to look away.

'I understand your name's Toby,' he said tersely. 'I take it that's short for Tobias?'

'Yes, it is,' replied Toby.'

Alice didn't understand what was going on between the two of them. They were like two powerful animals who had expected to feel nothing except antagonism towards each other, but who now found themselves drawn to each other in ways that they didn't quite understand.

Belatedly, she remembered she was meant to be phoning for the doctor. She went and found Frobisher, quickly explained what had happened, and asked for the name of the local doctor. Frobisher volunteered to make the call, leaving Alice free to return to the drawing-room. When she walked in, she found that Toby had already left.

'Did you send him away?' she demanded.

Dominic briefly looked amused. 'Do you mean, did I bodily throw him out? No, I didn't. I might be feeling better, but I don't think I'm capable of that just yet.'

'You know perfectly well what I mean,' Alice retorted. Then she ran her fingers shakily through her hair. 'I'm sorry, I didn't mean to shout at you. It's just that finding you like that scared me half to death. And now I don't understand what's going on——'

'Come and sit down,' he invited. 'I suppose you deserve a few explanations.'

She settled herself in the chair on the opposite side of the fireplace, and Dominic's mouth curled into a familiar, faintly mocking smile. 'Still keeping a safe distance away from me?' Then his tone altered slightly. 'Don't worry, I don't blame you for it. There's not much future in getting involved with a man like me.'

'A man like me'—he had used that phrase about himself once before, not long after she had first come to the Hall. Only, now she knew what he meant by it: a man who was incapable of giving a woman a child; someone who could only offer what was, in his mind, an empty relationship. Something inside her twisted sharply as she briefly shared the continuous underlying pain that must cause him.

Perhaps Dominic could read her face more easily than she had thought, because he suddenly moved restlessly.

'I thought you wanted to know about Toby?' he reminded her a little harshly.

Realising that he wanted—needed—to change the subject, she numbly nodded.

'I thought you would have guessed it by now,' he added.

'For a while, I thought I had,' Alice admitted. 'When I saw the likeness between you, I was sure he had to be your son. Then you told me——' She stopped instantly, aware that she had strayed back on to the old taboo subject.

Dominic didn't appear to be outwardly disturbed, though. Whatever his feelings on the subject, they were obviously strictly under control again now.

'I told you that there was no way I could have a son,' he said evenly. 'Anyway,' he went on with a wry smile, 'there's no more than ten years' difference between us in age. I might have been a precocious child, but I wasn't quite *that* advanced.'

'Then, who is Toby?'

'You'd have worked it out for yourself by now if you'd known my father's name. It was Tobias,' Dominic told her bluntly.

Alice stared at him in surprise. 'And Toby was named after him? He's your father's son? But that would make him——'

'My half-brother,' agreed Dominic. 'Illegitimate, but definitely a Seton.'

'And is it true? Did Toby tell you that himself?'

'He didn't have to. When I'm face to face with him, it's like looking in a damned mirror.'

Alice hesitated for a few moments, then said, 'How do you feel about it?'

'I haven't had a lot of time to get used to the idea yet,' he answered drily.

'And you really didn't know you had a half-brother? You never heard any rumours or gossip?'

Dominic gave a brief shrug. 'I've already told you, I've spent most of my life away from this house.'

'But you've been back for several months now,' she reminded him.

'Yes, I have, but Toby hasn't been around for most of that time. Apparently, he was in London, finishing a course in business administration. He's only been back a couple of weeks.'

'Do you suppose your brother, Robert, knew about it? After all, he lived here for several years before he died.'

'If he did, he never said a word to me about it. Not that that's very surprising. Robert was very possessive about Rossmore Hall and the estate. He wouldn't have wanted to admit the existence of an illegitimate half-brother who might possibly have some claim to a part of it.'

'Oh' said Alice, startled. That aspect hadn't occurred to her before. 'You mean, Toby might be entitled to part of your inheritance?'

'I really don't know,' replied Dominic, suddenly sounding very tired. 'I suppose it's a legal problem that'll have to be gone into at some time. Right now, though, my head aches so bloody much that I can't think straight about anything any more.'

'The doctor will be here soon,' she assured him. 'You'd better just sit quiet until he gets here.'

But Dominic didn't even seem to be listening to her any longer. He had settled back in the chair and closed his eyes, and he didn't move or speak again until the doctor arrived.

To Alice's intense relief, after a thorough physical examination the doctor pronounced that Dominic didn't have any serious injuries. His ribs were bruised, but fortunately not broken, and the cut on his forehead needed only two small stitches after it had been cleaned. The doctor left him some tablets that would dull the pain in his head and ribs, told him to stay in bed for at least a couple of days, and promised to call back in the morning to see how he was doing.

After the doctor had gone, Alice and Frobisher tried to persuade Dominic to go to bed. He announced that he was perfectly comfortable in the chair, though, and simply closed his eyes when they tried to argue with him. In the end, Alice fetched a blanket, while Frobisher made up the fire, and they left him there to sleep off the worst of the after-effects of his accident. Frobisher promised to keep an eye on him during the night, and Alice finally trailed up to bed, feeling totally shattered by the events of the last couple of days.

Against all expectations, she slept soundly, probably because she was completely exhausted. In the morning, she opened her eyes, yawned sleepily, then suddenly remembered everything that had happened yesterday. Grabbing her dressing-gown, she pulled it on and then hurried downstairs.

Reaching the drawing-room, she anxiously pushed open the door and then stopped dead. The chair where Dominic had spent the night was empty. Had he gone up to bed? Was he all right?

She turned round, and nearly bumped into Frobisher. 'Where is he?' she asked urgently.

Frobisher's face wore a distinctly disapproving expression. 'He's gone out for a walk with the dogs.'

'A walk?' she echoed disbelievingly. 'But he should be in bed, resting! Is the man mad?'

'Lord Rossmore said he needed some fresh air,' Frobisher said stiffly. 'I reminded him of the doctor's orders, but he said——' He hesitated, and his mouth set into an even more disapproving line. 'I can't recall his exact words, but they were along the lines that I should stop interfering and mind my own business.'

'Then he's obviously feeling better this morning,' Alice said drily.

'That was my conclusion, too,' agreed Frobisher.
'But the doctor will be here later, to give a more
informed opinion. By the way,' he went on, 'that young
man's waiting for you in the library. He arrived a little
while ago, and I told him you were still in bed, but he
said he would wait.'

'Young man?' echoed Alice. Then her face cleared.
'Oh—you mean Toby Collins? Has he been waiting
long?'

'Only a few minutes.'

'Then I'd better go and see him.'

Forgetting that she was still bare-footed and wearing
only a nightdress and open dressing-gown, she quickly
made her way to the library. As she walked through the
door, Toby turned from studying the shelves of books,
and an appreciative smile lifted the corners of his
mouth. It was so unnervingly reminiscent of Dominic
that Alice instantly flushed.

'If you walk around like that every morning, you
must drive Lord Rossmore nearly wild,' he told her, his
grin widening.

Flustered, Alice drew her dressing-gown more tightly
around her and secured it with the belt. 'I certainly
don't! Anyway,' she went on, 'isn't that a rather formal
way of addressing your half-brother?'

Toby went very still for a few moments. 'He admitted
that's who I am?' he said at last.

'He could hardly deny it. Anyone looking at the two
of you together could see there was a blood-tie.'

'He's never acknowledged it before.'

'That's not very surprising, since he didn't even know
you existed.'

'How could he not know?' Toby retorted a little
angrily. 'His brother, Robert, certainly knew about me.
Although he made it very clear that he didn't want

any contact between us,' he added rather grimly.

'Robert might well have known, but he never told Dominic. When you popped up at that medieval banquet, it was the first inkling Dominic had of your existence.' She gave a faint smile. 'I think it fairly knocked him for six. Why did you come that night? Out of sheer devilment?'

'Something like that,' Toby admitted reluctantly.

'And why are you here this morning?'

Toby looked as if he didn't really want to answer that question. 'To see if he's all right,' he rather grudgingly admitted, after a long pause.

Alice nodded in satisfaction. 'It's good that you care.'

'And there are a couple of things I wanted to tell him.'

'What kind of things?'

'That he needn't worry, I'm not going to turn this whole thing into a major scandal. There won't be any embarrassing court cases, with the illegitimate son trying to claim a share of the family loot, and a whole lot of skeletons being dragged out of the closet.'

'I don't think he ever thought you'd do anything like that,' Alice said quietly.

'Didn't he?' Toby looked momentarily puzzled. 'Why not?'

'Because the two of you are more alike than you even realise yet.' She smiled at him. 'Why don't you come back and see him in a couple of days, when he's feeling better? You've probably got a lot to talk about. And I think it would be good for him to have you around. He's rather short of people who are close to him.'

'He's got you, hasn't he?'

Toby's blunt statement made her pulses skip a beat. Then she took a deep breath and shook her head.

'No. Whatever you're thinking—you're wrong.'

He looked at her shrewdly. 'Am I?'

'Yes,' she said firmly. 'I work for him. That's all.' She glanced at her watch. 'I'd better go and get dressed, I've got a lot to get on with.'

'OK, I can take a hint.' He walked over to the door, then paused. 'But since everyone's suddenly being so truthful with each other, perhaps it's about time you started being honest, too. You're in love with my half-brother—and from what I've seen, that's a good thing. I think you're exactly the right person for him, Alice.'

Toby left after delivering that small bombshell, and Alice stood in the middle of the library, quietly shivering. Why had Toby actually had to say it out loud? Until now, she had successfully managed to convince herself it hadn't happened. It didn't look as if she was going to be able to run away from the truth any longer, though. She shivered again, and wondered what on earth she was going to do.

She made her way slowly upstairs and, as she took a long shower, she finally reached a decision. She would stay here for a couple more days, until Dominic was fully recovered. Then she would leave. It was the best decision—the *only* decision—under the circumstances.

Once she was dressed, she went back downstairs and phoned her mother to tell her she would be back home by the end of the week. Her mother was obviously surprised by the news, but tactful enough not to ask any questions. All the while Alice was talking to her, she could hear the twins in the background, playing what sounded like a very noisy game, and her heart contracted. She ached to be with them, and was only consoled by the thought that it would be just a couple more days before she was back with them for good. I'll never leave them again, she told herself fiercely, not for this long; and she spun out the conversation with her mother for as long as she could, listening hungrily to the childish chatter and yells of delight that nearly drowned out her mother's voice at times.

When she at last reluctantly put down the receiver, the silence of Rossmore Hall closed in around her, and she realised all over again just how empty this house seemed. Then she thought of Dominic spending the rest of his life in this emptiness, and a shaft of such sharp pity shot through her that she had to close her eyes momentarily.

The rest of the day turned out to be extraordinarily difficult to get through, and she soon began to wish she had just left straight away. She could hardly walk out on Dominic without any warning, though. His life was in enough of a turmoil at the moment; it wouldn't be fair of her to add to it.

Fortunately, she didn't actually have to see him. According to Frobisher, he came back from his walk far more tired that he would admit, and went directly up to his room to rest. Frobisher had then taken him up a hot drink that was laced with a couple of Mrs Frobisher's sleeping pills. A quarter of an hour later, Frobisher came back down to report, with some satisfaction, that 'His lordship was sleeping like a baby.'

Alice worked hard through the afternoon and into the evening. She wanted everything to be completely up to date by the time she finally left. She had her supper on a tray in the drawing-room, and then decided to have an early night.

She was just about to get up when Dominic walked through the doorway, scowling darkly.

'Who put those damn sleeping pills in my drink?' he demanded.

'When you ignored the doctor's orders about staying

in bed, Frobisher decided he'd better do something about it. And he did the right thing,' Alice added. 'You look much better now you've had a good sleep.'

'He'd better not try anything like that again,' Dominic growled ungratefully. 'Butlers aren't irreplaceable.'

Alice gave a faint grin. 'I think Frobisher probably is.'

He didn't smile back at her. Instead, his dark gaze fixed on her with an odd, hungry look that made her nerves suddenly twitch.

'I wasn't sure that you'd still be here when I came down.'

'Why shouldn't I be?' she asked a little uneasily.

'Because I keep getting the feeling that you're on the point of running away from me.'

That was so near to the truth that she had to look away from him. Was this the right time to tell him that she planned to do exactly that in a couple of days? No, she decided unsteadily, she just didn't feel up to it right now. She would tell him in the morning.

Dominic stretched himself out in the chair, then suddenly yawned. 'Damn those pills,' he said irritably. 'I still feel half asleep.'

'I'll leave you,' she said, getting up. 'Then you can take a nap.'

'No!'

That single, terse instruction was enough to send her straight back into the chair. Why did she always do what this man ordered? she wondered with a mixture of annoyance and unease. She had always prided herself on having a mind of her own, but when he was around, she seemed to give in without even a struggle.

'Toby called by this morning,' she said at last, trying to fill the silence that had suddenly stretched between them.

'What did he want?'

'To make sure that you were all right.'

Dominic's eyes flickered briefly, and she had the impression that he was pleased.

'Anything else?' he asked, just a little too casually.

'He wanted you to know that he—he doesn't want anything from you,' Alice went on, choosing her words carefully. 'He isn't going to announce to the world that he's a Seton, or make any sort of claim on the estate.'

'Mmm.'

Dominic's non-committal comment made her look up at him. 'Is that all you've got to say about it?' she asked a trifle sharply.

'For now—yes.' And from the tone of his voice, she knew he wouldn't be drawn any further on the subject. Nor did he make any effort to do anything else, though. He didn't move, didn't speak. He simply sat there, gazing thoughtfully at the flames dancing up from the grate.

Alice stared at him edgily. 'What are you thinking about?' she blurted out at last.

He turned and fixed his gaze back on her again, his eyes glittering darkly now.

'I was wondering where you and I went from here,' he said slowly.

Alice immediately wished she hadn't asked that question. 'We don't go anywhere,' she said shakily.

'Don't we?'

His softly spoken comment sent her pulses racing.

'You don't intend to get married,' she reminded him carefully. 'And I'm not looking for—any other kind of relationship.'

'You mean that you're the sort who always holds out for a wedding ring?' Dominic shook his head. 'I'm not

sure that I believe that, Alice. I think you could be open
to persuasion on the subject.'

Terrified of the form that 'persuasion' might
take—and her ability to hold out against it—Alice
froze.

'But you're right, I don't intend ever to marry,' he
went on. 'Nor will I ever change my mind about it. If
you can't have children, there just doesn't seem any
point.'

Alice's pulses were thundering away at top speed
now. 'You're absolutely certain you're—sterile?' She
stumbled awkwardly over that one short word that was
so incredibly difficult to get out. 'There couldn't have
been a mistake?'

Dominic's mouth set in a grim line. 'When you get a
verdict like that, you don't just take someone's word for
it. You get a second, a third and a fourth opinion. It's
only when they all come out exactly the same that you
finally accept the bloody thing's true.'

'How did you find out?' she asked him in a subdued
voice.

At first, she thought he wasn't going to tell her. Then
he raised his head and began speaking in a low,
expressionless tone. 'I had a long-term relationship with
a girl I'd met at university. We talked about marriage,
but I didn't feel I was ready yet for that sort of
commitment. I told her if she ever became pregnant,
though, we'd get married. We'd been together for
nearly a year when I came down one morning and found
her crying. Finally, I got her to tell me the truth. It
turned out she loved me far more than I'd realised, and
she'd been trying to get pregnant for ages, so I'd keep
my promise to marry her. Only it hadn't happened. Her
period had just started again, so it meant another month
had gone by with no sign of a baby.' He frowned.

'At first, I was extremely angry at the way she'd tried to trick me. Then I began to feel sorry for her. She was so upset and terrified at the thought that she might be infertile. In the end, we arranged for her to have some tests.' Dominic's face became even more bleak. 'When the results of those tests came back, they definitely weren't what I'd been expecting. The doctors couldn't find anything wrong with Marianne. They suggested—very tactfully, of course—that there could be some kind of problem on my side.'

'That must have been hard to take,' Alice said quietly.

'At first, I wouldn't even listen to them,' he muttered moodily. 'And I was furious with Marianne for getting me into the situation in the first place. After a while we broke up, our relationship just couldn't take the strain. I couldn't forget about it, though. That sort of thing eats away at you day and night, you can never put it right out of your mind. In the end, I decided it would be better to know one way or the other, rather than having the uncertainty always hanging over me.' He shrugged. 'The tests didn't take long, and they were absolutely conclusive. It turned out that I've an extremely low sperm count. Everything works perfectly—but with no end result.'

Alice flinched at the note of pain in his voice. 'It's absolutely impossible for you to father a child?' she asked with aching sympathy.

'Doctors don't like to use a word like "impossible",' Dominic responded harshly. 'Their verdict was that I had no more than a chance in a million. And since those sort of odds were hardly likely to come up in my lifetime, no matter how often I slept with someone, they told me that it would be far better if I accepted right from the very start that it just wasn't going to happen.'

'There are other alternatives,' she suggested hesitantly, after a very long pause. 'You could always adopt.'

'No!' His answer was immediate, and it was the one she had been expecting, even though something inside her had still been hanging on to a thin thread of hope until the very last moment. 'No,' he repeated evenly, and with total finality.

Alice didn't even have to ask him why. She already knew. If he couldn't have children of his own, then he could never bring himself to accept anyone else's. The small flicker of hope that had been burning in her heart quietly died. At least she knew where she stood now. She loved her twin sons. She loved Dominic Seton—she was finally ready to admit that. But she couldn't have all three, she had to choose between them. Which meant that there wasn't any choice at all.

Wearily, she got to her feet. 'I'm going upstairs now,' she told him. 'And you were right about me leaving. I'll be gone by this time tomorrow.'

'Even though I don't want you to go?'

She didn't—couldn't—answer, but instead began to walk towards the door. She never heard him get to his feet, didn't even hear him silently move towards her. The first she knew of his closeness was the touch of his hands on her shoulders, whirling her round to face him. Then there was the hardness of his lips closing over hers, the tight grip of his arms locking her against him, and a hot, dizzy darkness that swept over her and engulfed her.

This time, there was no gentleness, just a stark hunger that he was willing her—forcing her—to share. His mouth moved ceaselessly on hers, probing and caressing in turn until she could hardly breathe; his body burned its desire against her until she shivered helplessly in response. He moved back just a fraction, so he could slide one hand between them. His fingers thrust their way under her jumper, under her bra, searching for and finding the highly responsive tip to her swollen breast, then rubbing it into instant hardness, so that a small groan sounded deep in her throat.

Pleasure rushed through her in small waves, and he pressed her more forcefully against him, then ruthlessly kept her there until they both shook with frustration at the thin barrier of clothes that kept them apart. Blindly, she was answering his kisses now, for these few moments oblivious to everything except an uncontrollable surge of love for this man. Then Dominic lifted his head, his eyes nearly black and a little wild, a dark flare of colour staining his cheekbones.

'Now tell me that you don't want me!' he challenged harshly.

She couldn't do it. She wasn't capable of telling him such a lie.

'I know I don't have much to offer you,' Dominic went on, his breathing still ragged but his voice quieter, softer now. 'No marriage. No children. But can't you love me a little for my own sake?' His gaze locked on to hers and seemed to see right through to her very soul. 'Stay with me, Alice.'

The uncharacteristic note of pleading in his voice cut through her like a knife. She would have given anything to have been able to give him what he wanted. Anything—except her children.

'I can't,' she said, her voice suddenly dull and lifeless. 'I *can't*.'

His grip had slackened slightly, as if he couldn't believe she had turned him down. Taking advantage of it, she tore herself free of his arms and stumbled blindly out of the room.

CHAPTER NINE

ALICE left Rossmore Hall that same night. There was no way she could stay there any longer. To her utter relief, Dominic didn't try to stop her. She didn't even see him as she threw her things into her case, ran down to the car and then drove off into the night.

Her mother was surprised to see her but, after one look at her daughter's drawn, colourless face, she was wise enough not to ask any questions. Alice went straight up to the twins' room, and sat there for ages. The two boys were both sound asleep, and her gaze stayed fixed on their dear, familiar faces as she told herself over and over that she had made the right decision—the only decision. More drained than she had realised, she eventually fell asleep right there, in the chair. She didn't open her eyes again until the morning, when she was woken up by whoops of delight from the twins, who were obviously thrilled to find their mum was back home.

It was a struggle to get through the next few days, but she somehow made it. She spent every spare minute she had with the twins, partly to make up for the time she had spent away from them, but mostly because it was only when she was with them that the painful ache of misery inside her eased a little.

Luckily, there was plenty to keep her occupied, and that helped. Apart from the demands of the twins, there was a lot of work to catch up on at the agency. Susie had run things very efficiently while she had been away, but there were several problems that needed her personal attention, and she applied herself diligently to dealing with them.

All the same, some moments were a lot harder to get through than others. There had been that first morning back at her mother's house, when she had walked into the drawing-room and seen Dominic's painting hanging on the wall. It had been like a punch in the stomach, and she had stood very still for a few moments, then turned and quickly walked out again. Nothing had been said, but the next time she had gone in there, the painting was no longer there. Then there was the telephone. Every time it rang, her pulses leapt and then raced, and she began to shake inside. She avoided answering it, but always hung around nearby until she found out who was on the other end. Then she would walk away, her nerves feeling so strung up that she felt they might snap at any moment.

Her mother's house, which she had always thought very comfortable, suddenly seemed small and rather cramped after the vast spaciousness of Rossmore Hall. Sometimes she felt horribly shut in; she would whip the twins into warm coats, hats and boots, then rush them out into the garden for a game, or take them for a walk. When she was with them, things would seem almost normal for a while. As soon as they were out of sight, though, everything would begin to fall apart again.

And there was something else she hadn't expected. She had only been at Rossmore Hall for a short time, and yet she missed it like crazy. The atmosphere that reeked of its long history, the feeling that it had been lived in for centuries by people who had loved and appreciated it, the endless small problems that cropped up every day and needed solving. She missed the sight of Frobisher stalking along the corridors with his nose in the air, and his sharp eyes missing absolutely nothing. She even missed the damned dogs! But, most of all, she missed Dominic Seton. It was so hard to accept that they were going to follow separate paths for the rest of their lives.

At the end of the second week, Alice came down one evening after putting the twins to bed, slumped into the chair, and then realised that her mother was looking at her with an uncharacteristically impatient expression.

'Alice, why don't you simply pick up the phone and talk to him?' she said bluntly.

'Talk to whom?' Alice asked, deliberately pretending not to understand what her mother was getting at.

'The man whose painting I'm not allowed to have on the wall, because you turn white at just the sight of it!' her mother answered. 'If he's missing you half as much as you're missing him, then it shouldn't be too hard to straighten out any misunderstandings. Just try *talking* to each other.'

'It's not that simple,' Alice muttered.

'Isn't it? Are you sure you're not creating problems that don't really exist?'

'Oh, they exist all right!' came Alice's instant and bitter retort. 'They're upstairs right now, asleep in bed!'

Her mother frowned. 'The twins?'

'Yes, the twins. You want to know what the problem is? Then I'll tell you. Dominic Seton can't have children of his own, but he won't accept anyone else's.'

After a shocked silence, her mother slowly shook her head. 'It must be hard for a man to come to terms with something like that. But perhaps if he met the twins——'

'He doesn't even know anything about them,' Alice cut in rather abruptly.

'You didn't tell him?' Her mother sounded slightly incredulous.

'What was the point? He'd already made his views on the subject perfectly clear. What was I meant to do? Just dump the twins and go off with him? Have a good time while it lasted, and to hell with everything else?'

'I don't think he would have expected you to do that.' Her mother's tone was unexpectedly sharp. 'And I think you should at least have told him the truth.'

'What difference would it have made?' Alice demanded. 'If he can't have his own kids, then he doesn't want someone else's. That's something that isn't going to change, so where does that leave me? I'll tell you,' she went on, 'it leaves me right here, trying to get on with my life as best I can. There's no point in ringing him or going to see him, because there's no way that we could ever work things out between us.'

Her mother didn't say anything more after that, for which Alice was grateful. Even talking about Dominic was a strain. She was only going to get through this if she didn't think about him, or talk about him; if she could somehow keep him locked right out of her life.

Although it was March now, there were a couple of inches of snow at the weekend, and no let-up in the freezing cold weather. Saturday afternoon, the twins clamoured non-stop to go out and play in the snow. Since her mother had gone out to visit a friend, Alice finally gave in to their pleas. Bundling them up warmly, she let them loose in the garden to let off some of their endless supply of energy. Pulling on an old coat and scarf, she went out to join them, and after a fast and furious game of snowballs she started to make a snowman for them. There wasn't really enough snow, but the twins didn't care. They rushed around, scooping up handfuls of snow and dumping it in a heap so she could make the body, and she was just carefully moulding it into a round ball when she realised the twins had gone unusually quiet.

She glanced up, and found they were both standing still and staring towards the house.

'Come on, how about getting some more snow?' she said cheerfully. Then, when neither of them moved, she finally twisted round to see what had caught their attention.

When she saw the tall, dark man standing at the end of the path that led into the garden, she went as quiet and still as the twins.

'Mummy?' said Paul uncertainly, as Dominic began to walk towards them.

'It's all right, sweetheart,' she assured them soothingly. 'It's a friend of Mummy's. Go and play for a few minutes while I talk to him.'

'Snowman,' James reminded her, with a disapproving frown.

'I'll finish it in a minute,' she promised. 'Find me some more snow, so we can make him nice and big.'

The twins enthusiastically toddled off, and Alice finally found the courage to look at Dominic's face.

He was very white, and there was a strange look in his eyes. For a moment, she thought he was simply going to turn round and walk away without saying anything at all. Then his mouth set into a grim line.

'No wonder it was so hard to get you to talk about your private life,' he grated, with a touch of contempt. 'I should have guessed it was because you had something you wanted to hide.'

Alice glared at him furiously. 'I'm not ashamed of having two beautiful children!'

'No?' he challenged. 'Then how come you never once mentioned them?'

'It's something I don't tell employers unless they specifically ask,' she answered, fighting to keep her voice crisp and impersonal. 'You'd be surprised how much prejudice there still is against women with young children. Employers automatically assume you're always going to be taking time off to cope with illness or some domestic crisis.'

'And that's how you thought of me? As your *employer*?'

'Yes—at least, at first. And then there were—other reasons——' Alice's voice trailed away. She shouldn't have to go into those reasons, she thought to herself with a sudden burst of resentment. He knew them as well as she did. 'Anyway, it was none of your business,' she finished defiantly.

'None of my business?' Dominic echoed in disbelief. 'How the hell can you say that?' He abruptly stopped, as if he didn't trust himself to say any more.

Alice glanced at the twins, who had lifted their heads uncertainly as they heard the raised voices.

'Don't shout! They don't like it, and I won't have you coming here and upsetting them.'

'If they get upset that easily, then perhaps I'd better leave,' Dominic told her grimly. 'Because they most definitely wouldn't like watching what I'd like to do to you right now!'

'Then go,' she muttered to him. 'I don't want you here, poking your nose into my private affairs.'

His dark eyes hardened. 'I can appreciate the fact that you don't want me hanging around. If their father came home unexpectedly, it would be a bit difficult to explain what I was doing here, wouldn't it?' And, while Alice was still staring at him with a shocked expression, he went on savagely, 'I once told you that you were an old-fashioned girl, Alice. But I was wrong. There's another, far less pleasant name to describe you.'

And, with that, he wheeled round and strode off. Alice stared after him until he had disappeared from sight, and it wasn't until James tugged at her coat that she slowly came back to reality.

'Finish the snowman?' he pleaded. Then he looked rather surprised—and a little indignant—when she suddenly scooped him up and gave him a long, hard, and slightly desperate hug.

That evening, when the twins were in bed, her mother gave her a thoughtful look. 'The boys were telling me an interesting story while I was giving them their bath,' she remarked at last. 'It was pretty garbled, but it was all about a man who came in and stopped you building their snowman. They were pretty indignant about the whole thing,' she added a little drily.

Alice sighed. 'I suppose you'd have found out about it sooner or later. It was Dominic Seton.'

'And he saw the twins?' guessed her mother.

'He certainly did,' Alice confirmed rather grimly.

'And?'

'He didn't stick around for too long.' Alice lifted her head and stared directly at her mother. 'I told you he wouldn't.'

'The poor man was probably in a state of shock,' her mother said reasonably.

Alice conveniently pushed the memory of Dominic's white face out of her mind. 'The "poor man" has got an absolutely cast-iron nervous system,' she retorted. 'You're just prejudiced in his favour because you adore his paintings.' She got to her feet. 'I'm going to bed.'

But, as usual, she couldn't sleep. In the morning, she wandered down looking bleary-eyed, and only picked at her breakfast.

'Why don't you go and have a long soak in the bath?' suggested her mother. 'You might end up looking vaguely human again.'

'Thanks a lot,' muttered Alice, with a grimace. 'It's nice to have a sympathetic mother!'

But she obediently went back upstairs and climbed tiredly into the bath. She spent over an hour soaking in the hot, scented water, and then leisurely washed and dried her hair.

Squeaky clean and smelling delicious, she went downstairs again, just in time to see her mother hurriedly putting down the phone. As always, Alice's pulses gave a painful twitch. 'Anyone important?' she asked, rather too casually.

'Oh—no—just a friend,' answered her mother, slightly evasively. Then she glanced at her watch. 'I think we'll have an early lunch.'

'It's Sunday,' Alice reminded her. 'There's no hurry. We've nothing to do for the rest of the day.'

'I thought we'd go out for a couple of hours this afternoon. The twins are so full of energy that they'll probably wreck the place if they're kept cooped up all day.'

Alice glanced out of the window. 'It's absolutely freezing out there, and it looks as if it's going to snow again. Where on earth will we go?'

'We'll find somewhere,' her mother replied briskly. 'Come on, let's get something to eat.'

Lunch was prepared, eaten and then cleared away at what seemed to Alice like record speed. Then she found herself being bundled into her mother's car, along with the twins.

'Where are we going?' she demanded.

'I thought we'd just drive around for a while.' Her mother got behind the wheel and revved up the engine. 'We're bound to end up somewhere.'

Alice sighed. It was impossible to get a straight answer out of her mother when she was in one of these moods. Instead, she settled down on the back seat with the twins, and began playing a game with them to keep them occupied.

It was some time later before she glanced out of the window again. Then she frowned. This road looked uncomfortably familiar.

'I think we ought to turn back now,' she said rather abruptly. 'The twins are starting to get bored.'

'The twins are fine,' said her mother firmly. Then she put her foot down on the accelerator, and the car shot forward even faster.

Alice turned back to the boys, who were both clamouring for her to start playing the game again, but she couldn't concentrate. She knew this route, knew where it led. She consoled herself with the thought that her mother would soon be turning off, though. There wasn't the slightest possibility that they would be going the whole way.

Yet, to her astonishment—and utter disbelief—her mother eventually swung the car through the gates that led to Rossmore Hall.

'What are you doing?' she demanded incredulously.

'I'm doing something that I always promised myself I'd never do,' her mother said placidly. 'I'm interfering in your life.'

'Then just stop it!' Alice retorted. 'Turn round and take us home.'

But her mother drove steadily on, and soon the car

was pulling up before the front entrance of Rossmore Hall. Alice couldn't believe any of this was really happening, that she was actually here.

'Alice, get out,' instructed her mother. Still stunned, Alice automatically obeyed her. 'Boys—go with your mother,' she went on. The twins didn't need telling twice. They were fed up with being cooped inside the car, and they climbed out as quickly as they could.

Once the three of them were standing on the gravel drive, her mother put the car into gear and drove off.

'I must be dreaming,' Alice muttered, shaking her head dazedly as she watched the car disappearing into the distance. 'Either that, or my mother's gone a little crazy! What on earth made her do something like this?'

A few snowflakes were beginning to flutter down, and she shivered. She would have to ring for a taxi to get them home. But the only phone for miles around was at Rossmore Hall. She turned apprehensively towards the front entrance, and then discovered that the door was already open. Moreover, Dominic was standing there, silently watching them.

She somehow gathered herself together and caught hold of a twin in each hand. There was nothing else for it—she would have to ask if she could use the phone.

Reluctantly, she went up the steep steps, the twins manfully scrambling up beside her, until all three of them were standing in front of Dominic. James stared at the tall, dark man, and then suddenly seemed to remember that he had seen him before. Unexpectedly, he grinned, and Paul's mouth immediately stretched into a similar huge smile. If something—or someone—was all right with James, then it was all right with him, too.

Dominic smiled back, a warm smile which astonished her. Then he switched his attention to her, and she felt a familiar rush of colour to her face.

'I'm sorry, I know we shouldn't be here,' she got out in a shaky voice. 'But my mother brought us here and just dumped us on your doorstep. I don't know why she did such a crazy thing. I suppose she was trying to tell me that it's about time I got a few things sorted out, but she doesn't understand, she doesn't know all the facts. I mean,' she blundered on, 'there's nothing *to* sort out, is there?'

'On the contrary,' Dominic said calmly. 'I'd have thought there's a great deal to get straightened out. And I know exactly why your mother brought you here. It's because I phoned her this morning, and asked her if she'd do precisely that.'

Alice gaped at him. 'You—what?'

'I was very angry when I left you the other day. I kept thinking of the way you'd behaved when you were with me, the way you'd kissed me, responded to me——' His eyes briefly gleamed. 'Then I started picturing you doing those same things with the twins' father, loving *him* while carrying on a casual affair with me. When I finally cooled off a little, though, I remembered you'd once told me that you lived with your mother. Something didn't add up. In the end, I decided to phone your mother. She's a charming woman,' he added. 'And *very* helpful. She soon straightened me out on several rather important matters.' He glanced up at the heavy sky. 'Don't you think you'd better come inside?' he went on conversationally. 'We can't stand out here and talk—it's going to start snowing hard in a couple of minutes.'

As she dazedly stumbled in after him, the twins stared around with fast-growing interest and approval.

This was the sort of place where you could play really good games. Then the two wolfhounds came loping into the entrance hall, their tails wagging lazily as they went over to inspect the two small newcomers.

Paul stared up uncertainly at the huge dog looming way over his head. 'Horse?' he questioned doubtfully.

'No, sweetheart,' said Alice, with an involuntary grin. 'It's a dog.'

Neither of the twins looked as if they quite believed her, but they patted and stroked whatever part of the wolfhounds they could reach, and the dogs obviously lapped up the attention. Alice watched a little anxiously. The dogs were so big; they could easily knock the boys over if they weren't careful.

Dominic noticed her sudden concern. 'Don't worry,' he told her quietly. 'Both the dogs are marvellous with kids. They're as gentle as lambs, despite their size. How about if we turn all four of them loose in the Great Hall? There's plenty of room for them all to run around and get to know each other.'

'I can't leave them on their own,' Alice said quickly. 'They've never been here before, they'll be frightened.'

'They don't look very frightened to me,' Dominic remarked drily. And it was true. The two boys were already heading off down the corridor, chasing after the wolfhounds. 'Anyway, Mrs Frobisher will keep an eye on them, to make sure they don't wander off and get lost.'

'I ought to stay with them,' she insisted stubbornly.

'Afraid of being alone with me?'

His soft challenge hit home because it was the truth.

'Well, I suppose it would be all right to leave them for just a few minutes——' she said reluctantly.

Dominic linked his hand firmly through hers and led her into the nearby drawing-room. 'We'll leave the door ajar so we can hear if there are any sudden yells for maternal attention.'

'I don't understand why you got my mother to bring me here,' Alice muttered uneasily, pulling her hand out of his and backing away from him a little.

'I know you don't. But we'll come to that later. First of all, there are a few things that *you* are going to tell *me*.'

'About what?'

'About those two, for a start. And I wouldn't mind knowing something about their father.'

'It's none——' she began hotly.

'Tell me again that it's none of my business, and I might begin to get rather angry,' Dominic warned. 'So, start at the beginning, Alice, and keep talking until you finally get to the end.'

His dark gaze was fixed on her intently, silently telling her that she didn't have any choice, that she was going to have to tell him the entire truth this time.

Alice slumped into a nearby chair, suddenly feeling very tired. 'It's the kind of story you often hear someone else tell,' she said at last. 'You think, that'll never happen to me, I'd never be that stupid. Then it *does* happen, and you realise just how easy it is to get caught, to be careless for just a few minutes and end up like so many other girls.' She paused, then went on, 'I was working as personal assistant to the managing director of a small London-based company. An important American client was coming over, and at the last moment my boss went sick. I was roped in to take over the social side of the visit. This client had never been to London before, and he wanted to see a couple of shows, do the rounds of the top nightclubs, visit the sights—the usual things.'

'What was his name?' asked Dominic quietly.

'Jerry,' she said, after a slight pause. 'Jerry Maitland.'

'What was he like?'

Alice shrugged. 'I don't really know.' Then she twisted her fingers together miserably. 'Does that sound awful? I suppose it does. But it's the truth. We never really talked, not about anything important. He was very charming, I remember that. And he was nice-looking. He seemed to enjoy his stay in London, he wanted to see absolutely everything. Then, on the night before he was due to fly back home, he said he'd just found out a friend of his was in town, and this friend had invited him to a party he was throwing that night. He wanted to take me, as a way of thanking me for taking such good care of him all week. I didn't really want to go, I was dead beat. Jerry insisted, though, so in the end I said I'd go for just a couple of hours.' She grimaced. 'The party turned out to be pretty wild. This friend of his had rented a large house, and it was crammed full of people. Everyone was packed together like sardines, it was very hot, and there wasn't anything to drink except champagne. I drank glassfuls of the stuff, trying to keep cool, which was pretty stupid because I'd had hardly anything to eat all day. Finally, my head got really woozy and I knew I couldn't take any more. I told Jerry I'd take a taxi home, so he could stay on and enjoy the rest of the party.'

'But he didn't go along with that idea?' guessed Dominic, a trifle grimly.

She shook her head. 'He insisted on taking me himself.' She stopped, took a deep breath, and then forced herself to go on again. 'He took me right up to my flat, then said he'd like to give me a goodbye kiss, since he was flying home the next day and wouldn't be seeing me again. But somehow that kiss turned into something else.' Alice lifted her shoulders helplessly. 'I haven't got any excuses for what happened. He didn't force me, I can't pretend that he did.' She gave a slightly bitter smile. 'There's a rather crude phrase for it. "He pushed all the right buttons". And I didn't put up much more than a token protest. I *wanted* to feel all those things he was making me experience. I was a twenty-one-year-old virgin, and I suddenly wanted to know what it was all about. For a few hours, I didn't care about anything except having a good time.'

Her gaze flickered up to Dominic, expecting to see a look of disgust or censure on his face. Instead, though, to her amazement, he simply looked angry.

'The man must have known you'd had too much to drink,' he growled. 'He had no right to take advantage of that fact.'

'Whether he did or not—it happened,' Alice said in a low voice. 'And it wasn't until I woke up in the morning with a terrific hangover that I really realised just what I'd done. Jerry had gone by then—although I was relieved at that. I didn't want to face anyone, and especially not him. I felt absolutely sick. I just couldn't believe I'd behaved like that, gone to bed with someone I didn't love, someone I didn't even know very well.'

'You wouldn't have done it if you'd been sober,' Dominic said with complete certainty.

'No, I wouldn't,' she admitted. 'But somehow that made it even worse. To get drunk, and then tumble into bed with the first man who laid hands on me.' She shuddered, remembering the deep sense of shame that had haunted her.

'What did you do?' prompted Dominic gently.

'I finally decided I'd have to try and forget about it, or it would drive me a little crazy. I'd get on with my life, and make sure it never, *ever* happened again.'

Her mouth twisted into a self-mocking smile. 'Only it was already too late for that sort of resolution. A few weeks later, I realised I was pregnant.' Her face became shadowed. 'It was the most awful day of my life. I really hit rock bottom then—and I stayed there until the twins were finally born.'

Dominic frowned. 'Didn't you get any sort of support or help from Maitland?'

'He didn't want to know,' Alice answered flatly. 'When I'd had the pregnancy confirmed, I knew I'd have to tell him about it. After all, he had the right to know, he *was* the father. At first, I was going to write. Then I thought the wrong person might open the letter and read it, so I decided to phone.'

'What was the response?'

'He said there was no way he could be the father.' Alice shook her head disbelievingly. 'When he said that, I wanted to hit him! Except I couldn't—he was three thousand miles away in America. Then he told me that he already had a wife and two kids—something he'd never mentioned while he was in London!—and that if I tried to cause trouble, I'd end up very sorry. He'd tell everyone I slept around all over the place, that there were at least half a dozen men who could be the father. When I said he couldn't possibly prove that, because it wasn't true, he just laughed. Then he said money talks, and it wouldn't be hard for him to produce witnesses who'd be willing to swear they'd been to bed with me.' She gave a small shudder. 'I couldn't believe he was the same charming man I'd known in London.'

'Sometimes charming men can be complete bastards underneath,' Dominic said tersely. Then he added, 'Did you ever consider an abortion?'

'I thought about it, but I knew I couldn't do it. Not for moral or religious grounds,' she added, 'I just knew

I wouldn't be able to go through with it when the time came. I had more or less decided to opt for adoption. I was so certain I just wanted to get the pregnancy over and done with and then get on with my life, forget the entire awful business. Then I took one look at the twins after they were born, and that was it. I was hooked. I knew that they were mine, that I loved them no matter who their father was, or how appallingly he'd treated me. No one was ever going to make me give them up.'

'You've never regretted that decision?'

'No,' she said without hesitation.

'And their natural father still refuses to acknowledge them?' There was a slightly tense note in Dominic's voice now.

'He's dead,' Alice answered simply. 'He was killed in a car crash just over a year ago. I wouldn't even have known, but I had a letter from his lawyers shortly afterwards warning me not to make any claim on Jerry's estate. They said I had absolutely no legal rights since his paternity could now never be proved.' Her dark eyes flashed. 'As if I would have asked for a single penny!'

'And you weren't at all upset by his death?' Dominic's gaze rested on her intently. 'He *was* the twins' father,' he reminded her.

'Not as far as I'm concerned,' Alice answered immediately. 'A child's father is the man who raises and loves them, who's there when they need him.'

'And do you think I could fill that role?'

His question briefly stunned her. 'But—you said you were against adoption,' she said rather shakily at last. 'It's why I had to leave. I knew you'd never be able to accept the twins.'

Dominic shook his head. 'You're wrong, Alice. When I said I was against adoption, it wasn't for the reasons

that you thought. I would have been perfectly happy to
adopt, but I didn't think I had the right to ask any
woman to accept someone else's children and give up all
hope of ever having any of her own.'

Alice's heart had almost stopped. 'But—I've already
got two children of my own,' she said slowly.

'Yes, my love, you have,' Dominic agreed. 'Which
makes my argument rather invalid.' He still looked very
tense. 'But could you live with the fact that you won't
have any more?'

'I could live with anything, as long as I had you,' she
told him without hesitation. 'And my mother always
brought me up to believe that nothing is impossible,' she
added with a faint smile. 'Remember—the doctors did
give you a chance in a million.'

'Don't count on it,' he warned her. 'I've tried to be
totally honest with you. In return, you've got to accept
the situation as it is, or we'll be in trouble right from the
start.' His eyes stared down into hers, and she could see
the sudden wave of doubt that swept over him. 'I don't
want to disappoint you,' he muttered fiercely.

'No matter what happens—or doesn't happen
—you'll never disappoint me. Don't you know that?'

'I might know it,' he answered huskily, after a brief
pause. 'But I think I need you to prove it to me!'

A second later, she was in his arms. The familiar
warmth of his mouth was druggingly sweet, the touch of
his hands left her aching for a more intimate fulfilment.
She curled closer to him, then gave a small sigh of
pleasure and satisfaction at his instant fierce response.
His hands fitted tightly into the small of her back,
gripping her with sudden need, and his lips told her over
and over of his love for her—and the promise of where
that love would lead. Then, groaning a little, he
reluctantly pushed her away from him.

'No more! Not unless you want me to do something quite outrageous right here and now, where everyone can walk in and see us!'

'You'd better get used to an audience. And to being interrupted at very inconvenient moments,' Alice told him. 'The twins have got into the habit of climbing into bed with me whenever they feel like a cuddle.'

'I dare say I'll learn to live with it,' Dominic said with cheerful resignation. 'Just as long as they don't intend to share our bed *all* the time,' he added huskily.

He had just begun to kiss her again when there was a flurry of movement from the doorway. They both turned round to find the twins staring at them rather suspiciously.

'I warned you about the audience!' Alice grinned. Then she added, 'I'm not sure that they entirely approve of you kissing me.'

'I'm afraid they're just going to have to get used to it,' Dominic said firmly. 'It's something that's going to happen very often.' Then he released her and walked over to the two small boys. 'I think it's about time we got to know each other,' he told them. He linked his hands through theirs and, rather bemusedly, they clung on to this tall, dark man who had so suddenly come into their lives, and who looked as if he might turn out to be rather interesting to know. 'Let's start by spending a couple of hours together, and see how it turns out.' Alice went to join them, but Dominic shook his head. 'No, it would be better if you waited here. Give us a chance to be on our own for a while.'

The twins toddled off with him, uncharacteristically quiet and with slightly anxious faces, and Alice felt her stomach begin to churn with nervousness. What if it didn't work out? What if——? Oh, stop it! she told herself firmly. It would work out. It *had* to.

The afternoon passed by incredibly slowly, and she paced anxiously up and down the drawing-room, somehow resisting the urge to rush off in search of them. Finally, she heard the sound of voices approaching, all three of them familiar. One was dark and unmistakably male, the other two were chattering away childishly, gabbling the half-formed sentences that it often took time and patience to decipher.

When they eventually came into the room, she saw that Paul was perched on Dominic's shoulders, while James was trotting alongside, confidently clutching his hand.

'Played with horses,' James informed her excitedly.

'Dogs,' Dominic corrected him, with a grin. 'You can see some real horses tomorrow. They're bigger—much bigger.'

James' eyes nearly popped out at the thought of something bigger than the wolfhounds.

'Come on, Paul,' added Dominic, 'down you come. Then you and James can go and have some tea. Mrs Frobisher's spent most of the afternoon making you something special.'

Alice stared at Dominic in astonishment as he easily swung Paul down from his shoulders. 'You can tell them apart?'

'Of course I can,' he replied, looking slightly surprised.

She shook her head. 'Then that makes you one of the three people in the world who can!'

'Jelly for tea?' asked Paul hopefully, trying to steer the conversation back to a more important subject.

'I've no idea,' Alice muttered. 'But on a day like today, absolutely anything's possible. Are you hungry?' When they both roared their assent, she laughed

out loud with sheer pleasure. 'Come on, then. I'll take
you along to the kitchen.'

With the twins finally seated at a table piled with
food, tucking in under Mrs Frobisher's watchful but
affectionate eye, Alice gave them a last loving look, and
then went back to Dominic.

He took her hands in his and pulled her a little closer.
'A few weeks ago, I was almost completely on my own,'
he told her drily. 'Now it looks as if I'm about to
acquire a wife, two sons, and a mother-in-law.'

'Do you think you can cope?' she teased, grinning,
and at the same time loving him for the way he had so
naturally referred to the twins as his sons.

'I don't think it'll be too difficult,' he assured her.
'But how do you feel about becoming Lady Rossmore?
And living in this great barn of a house?'

'I'm going to love every minute of it. So will the
twins. It's a marvellous place for children to grow
up.'

'Will you want to keep on working?' Dominic asked
her. 'I know how much time and effort you've put into
that agency of yours.'

'I don't know,' she confessed. 'I often feel guilty
about spending so much time away from the twins. It's
something I'll have to think about. But not right now,'
she added. 'All I can think about at the moment is
you!'

'Good,' he said, with some satisfaction. Then he
grinned. 'I'm not sure how Frobisher's going to take all
this. He found it hard enough to come to terms with the
dogs. Now he's going to have two small boys charging
round the place. He'll probably have a nervous
breakdown before the year's out.'

'Poor Frobisher,' said Alice sympathetically. 'We'll
all have to be extra nice to him, to make up for

it.'

'I'd rather you were extra nice to me,' murmured Dominic, nuzzling her neck. 'By the way, did I tell you about Toby?'

'Toby?' she echoed a little giddily. Then she remembered the young man who so resembled Dominic. 'Toby!' she exclaimed. 'You've seen him again?'

'Several times. I thought we ought to try and make up for all the years when we didn't know each other.'

'Then he definitely is your half-brother?'

'Yes. There's absolutely no doubt about it. There's a different name on his birth certificate, of course, but no one could look at him and deny he's a Seton.'

'How did you get on together?' asked Alice a trifle apprehensively.

Dominic grinned. 'Don't look at me like that, my love. I didn't beat him into the ground at our very first meeting! Mind you, things were a little shaky at the start,' he recalled. 'But once we got talking, it didn't take long to get things straightened out. And we've come to some rather satisfactory arrangements regarding the future.'

'Such as?'

'For a start, Toby's suggested a new site for my proposed golf and sports complex. It's far enough away from Amberleigh to keep the locals happy, but it'll still bring in a lot of revenue to the estate and provide plenty of new jobs. More than that, though, we've agreed that he'll take over the running of the Hall.'

'He'll what?' she squeaked.

'I'm a painter, not an administrator. And more than anything, I want to get back to my work. Toby's just finished a course in business administration, and he's got a lot of good, sound ideas for making the Hall more commercially viable without completely ruining it.

It makes sense for him to take over that side of things. And he'll live at the Hall, of course. He *is* a Seton—he's every right to be here.'

'*I* know that,' Alice retorted. 'I just never expected *you* to be so reasonable.'

'But I'm a very reasonable man,' he assured her. 'As long as I get what I want.' His hands moved purposefully, telling her very clearly what he wanted right now. 'It's still snowing hard,' he added. 'I should think there's very little chance of you getting home tonight. Or for several nights,' he went on more huskily.

Alice sighed with delight at the prospect. 'I hope it snows for weeks. But with the house full of dogs, boys and butlers, do you suppose we'll ever get a moment to ourselves?'

'There are ninety-five rooms in Rossmore Hall,' Dominic reminded her, gently caressing the warm swell of one breast with obvious pleasure. 'We ought to be able to find one where we won't be disturbed.'

She stirred appreciatively under his touch. 'The twins have had an exciting day. I think I ought to put them straight to bed once they've finished their tea.'

'I'll help you. And afterwards, I'd rather like to put *you* to bed, Alice,' he murmured. His mouth slid down the silky curve of her neck. 'Do you think that sounds like a good idea?'

She hid her face against his shoulder. 'I can't think of anything I'd like more.'

'Mmm. For an old-fashioned girl, you're showing a rather shocking eagerness to jump into bed with me.' He suddenly shuddered, and then laughed as he caught hold of her hand. 'Alice! Old-fashioned girls aren't supposed to do things like that!'

'Aren't they?' she said demurely. 'Then perhaps we'd

better put the twins to bed, and you can show me all the other things that old-fashioned girls aren't meant to do.'

Dominic's dark eyes gleamed. 'It'll be my pleasure. And yours, too,' he promised huskily.

And the silence of Rossmore Hall closed around them as they exchanged one more slow, lingering kiss that sealed their commitment to each other.

Harlequin Temptation dares to be different!

Once in a while, we Temptation editors spot a romance that's truly innovative. To make sure *you* don't miss any one of these outstanding selections, we'll mark them for you.

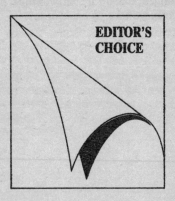

EDITOR'S CHOICE

When the "Editors' Choice" fold-back appears on a Temptation cover, you'll know we've found that extra-special page-turner!

THE

Temptation

EDITORS

Harlequin American Romance

Romances that go one step farther...
American Romance

Realistic stories involving people you can relate to and care about.

Compelling relationships between the mature men and women of today's world.

Romances that capture the core of genuine emotions between a man and a woman.

Join us each month for four new titles wherever paperback books are sold.
Enter the world of American Romance.

Amro-1

Harlequin Presents

Coming Next Month

Available in February wherever paperback books are sold, or through Harlequin Reader Service:

In the U.S.
901 Fuhrmann Blvd.
P.O. Box 1397
Buffalo, N.Y. 14240-1397

In Canada
P.O. Box 603
Fort Erie, Ontario
L2A 5X3

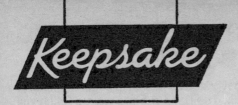

 Harlequin Books

You're never too young to enjoy romance. Harlequin for you . . . and Keepsake, young-adult romances, destined to win hearts, for your daughter.

Pick one up today and start your daughter on her journey into the wonderful world of romance.

Two new titles to choose from each month.